You know you have hit upon the right the planned lesson for the day to return to *Aloha Shorts*, mobbing the Bamboo Ridge Press website to hear more. *The Best of Aloha Shorts* collects together authors, actors, and musicians that students and other Bamboo Ridge fans may now enjoy on their earbuds and read all in one place. I love this resource! Plus, producer, performer, and author commentary offers a window into production of this expertly curated radio program. Students, take note. *Aloha Shorts*, long may you run. Long may you run.

Claire Gearen
Educator
Hawai'i Public Schools

The 30-minute weekly radio program *Aloha Shorts* became destination listening for anyone interested in Hawai'i stories and literature. Over four years it became a major jewel in HPR's local-programming crown.

Michael Titterton
Former President & General Manager
Hawai'i Public Radio

These are amazing, amusing, and compelling stories, a great avenue to the public humanities and the life of the mind they represent. The diverse topics and writings, performed thematically for *Aloha Shorts*, connect us to ideas about family and community, engage us in daily dilemmas and challenges, and make us richer human beings by their knowing telling. They become "human-ties"—holding us in their wisdom, civic virtues, and civility, and wearing those cool aloha shorts. The Hawai'i Council for the Humanities is proud to have supported this storytelling experience. I'm so glad that through this book the stories can continue to support us all.

Bob Buss
Executive Director
Hawai'i Council for the Humanities

THE BEST OF
AL HA
SHORTS

THE BEST OF ALOHA SHORTS

edited by
Sammie Choy, Craig Howes, Phyllis S.K. Look

Bamboo Ridge Press

ISBN 978-0-910043-98-4

This is issue #112 of *Bamboo Ridge, Journal of Hawai'i Literature and Arts* (ISSN 0733-0308).

Published by Bamboo Ridge Press
Printed in the United States of America

Bamboo Ridge Press is a member of the Community of Literary Magazines and Presses (CLMP).

Typesetting and design by Jui-Lien Sanderson
Photographs by Sammie Choy
"*Aloha Shorts* Theme Song" and "Honolulu City Lights" are reprinted by permission of the creators.

Bamboo Ridge Press is a nonprofit, tax-exempt corporation formed in 1978 to foster the appreciation, understanding, and creation of literary, visual, or performing arts by, for, or about Hawai'i's people. This publication was made possible with support from the National Endowment for the Arts (NEA), and the Hawai'i State Foundation on Culture and the Arts (SFCA), through appropriations from the Legislature of the State of Hawai'i (and grants by the NEA). Additional support for Bamboo Ridge Press public events provided by the Hawai'i Council for the Humanities.

Bamboo Ridge is published twice a year. For subscription information, back issues, or to purchase books, please visit **www.bambooridge.com**.

Bamboo Ridge Press
P.O. Box 61781
Honolulu, HI 96839-1781
808.626.1481
brinfo@bambooridge.com

CONTENTS

Michael Titterton
Hawai‘i Public Radio[*]

Books have been having a tough time of it lately, as flashier and "handier" conduits for the written word have been developed. Radio, as a unique conveyer of the spoken word, has been slugging out this battle for much longer. Every new tech wave, from television to podcast, has required radio to look to its roots, remember what it does uniquely well, and then learn to do it better.

And it turns out that one of the services that radio can provide better than any other medium is one of the very oldest—perhaps the most ancient of all, so old it's part of our DNA. It can draw its community around the campfire, and against the silence and the warming glow, enable it to tell its stories.

Hawai‘i Public Radio (HPR) takes this responsibility seriously. One of the most original and successful examples of HPR's commitment to this idea has been *Aloha Shorts*, a collaboration between Bamboo Ridge Press and HPR, masterminded by co-producers Phyllis S.K. Look, Sammie Choy, and Craig Howes. The basic idea was simple enough: local stories written by local authors, read by local actors (sometimes the authors themselves) before a local audience, and then broadcast over our local public radio network. Add Phyllis's and Sammie's stagecraft, a house band, a charismatic emcee, and the irresistible lure of free admission and cookies, and . . . well, for the first couple of months it was hard to get anyone to take any notice.

BUT (and this is where public radio always scores) everyone persevered, none more resolutely nor determinedly than the producers. Before very long the seats were filling up and the broadcast audience was growing—the experience of bearing witness to Hawai‘i telling its own stories to its own people proved irresistible, and the show began developing cult status. Would-be audience members spilled out onto Kāheka Street, inconveniencing traffic. The 30-minute weekly radio program, engineered by Jason Taglianetti, became destination listening for anyone interested in Hawai‘i stories and literature. Over four years it became a major jewel in HPR's local-programming crown.

I'll always be grateful to Phyllis, Sammie, Craig, and Bamboo Ridge for doing so much to help HPR live up to its full potential, during these transient and tweetful times, as a keeper of our community's cultural flame. This fine collection, drawn from the series, is a fitting tribute.

---

[*] Michael Titterton was the President and General Manager of Hawai‘i Public Radio during the years when *Aloha Shorts* was on the air.

Cedric Yamanaka
host, writer, and performer

Aloha.

That's the way we opened every show.

Hawai'i needed something like *Aloha Shorts*. As we all know, our island home is blessed with world-class writers, actors, and musicians. Hawai'i Public Radio and Bamboo Ridge Press recognized this and took a chance. They gave these good folks a place to show their stuff, a playing field for them to do their thing in front of a live audience.

The format of the show was pretty simple. Local actors and actresses came into the Atherton Studio and read poetry and fiction by local authors. Throw in some awesome musicians to set the mood and we were good to go.

As host, my job was to stay out of their way and let the performers shine. I can't begin to tell you the number of times I sat amazed, watching some of these artists perform live and in person.

Our beginnings were very humble. In the early days, we'd struggle to find an audience. Some nights, we had maybe five people in the house. An intimate crowd, no question.

Years passed. Slowly but surely, things changed and the show evolved. Crowds started getting larger. Lines gathered outside the studio. We dedicated shows to food, love, ghosts, the economy, the elderly, and holidays. We did our hundredth show in front of a packed house. It was hard work, but rewarding.

I am thankful to every single person who appeared on *Aloha Shorts*, visited us at a taping, listened to us on the radio, or contributed to its success. It truly was an honor to serve as your host.

Aloha!

Origin Story: *Aloha Shorts*
Mark Lutwak
founding director

In 2004, I was serving as artistic director of Honolulu Theatre for Youth. I was coming into daily contact with talented local actors and local writers. I was trying to convert the latter into playwrights. Many of these writers had a substantial body of poetry and prose marked by a sense of "strong voice." To my eye and ear, even if they weren't playwrights, they were profoundly aware of how this work sounded aloud. Conversations with Michael Titterton and Jeff Ilardi at Hawai'i Public Radio led to a simple plan. We would have local actors read this work in front of a live audience, record it, and broadcast it. My time, and that of the actors, was pretty crazy. So we hammered out a simple formula: we would only do literature published by *Bamboo Ridge*. They had already done the legwork of seeking out and editing the best of the best. This way, I would not have to plow through submitted manuscripts. We would read the work "straight." We would not take the time to "dramatize" the material. This way, the actors and I would not have to spend significant time rehearsing. We would let the talent of the writers and actors speak for themselves. We mixed in local singer/songwriters and added Cedric Yamanaka as a host. We had a show. When life moved me from O'ahu to "O'hio," I passed it on to Phyllis, Sammie, and Craig. I understand that they took it to a whole new level.

The Best of Aloha Shorts — A History and an Explanation
Sammie Choy, Craig Howes, Phyllis S.K. Look

When the editors of *Bamboo Ridge* asked if we would be interested in editing a *Best of Aloha Shorts* anthology, we agreed almost immediately. As the co-producers from late 2008 until 2012 of the show, we welcomed the opportunity to revisit the poems, stories, and performances, and to create a collection that would let readers experience what we felt were some of the show's highlights.

This introduction provides some information about what the program was, how it began, how we became its co-producers, how we put the shows together, and why eventually we brought *Aloha Shorts* to a close. We have organized the contents around some of the themes we explored on the show. We also supply directions to online resources that let readers hear the broadcast performances of the poems and stories featured in this anthology. The result is a collection of some of the finest work published by Bamboo Ridge Press, further enriched by the artists who brought the writing to life for listeners every week.

Origins, Transitions, and SOPs

As Mark Lutwak, the show's founding producer, indicates in his brief note, *Aloha Shorts* began in 2004, with a simple but compelling vision. Each week, the show would present radio listeners with Hawai'i literature performed by Hawai'i actors and recorded before a live audience. The pieces were all from Bamboo Ridge Press, publishers since 1978. Cedric Yamanaka was the host; musical guests might appear. To avoid extensive rehearsal time, the performances would be "straight"—just the text. And except for Jason Taglianetti, the HPR staff recording engineer, everyone involved was a volunteer.

When Mark had to leave the show, after some discussion between Bamboo Ridge and HPR, founding co-editor Darrell H.Y. Lum offered Phyllis Look the opportunity to produce *Aloha Shorts*. She agreed, but asked if Sammie Choy and Craig Howes could be co-producers, since what Phyllis imagined would be more than one person could handle, and Sammie and Craig both had backgrounds in the Hawai'i literary and dramatic scenes. Mark, Bamboo Ridge, and HPR had no objections, and the new team began planning its first shows, which were taped in November of 2008, and broadcast in early 2009.

The three-producer model allowed for a division of labor and a collaborative creative approach. Some parameters were set—*Aloha Shorts* would still be a half-hour weekly show featuring live readings of Hawai'i literature taped in HPR's Atherton Studio for eventual broadcast. But how to approach the task? In our first few weeks as producers we made several decisions that held good for the next three-and-a-half years. First, we ensured Cedric Yamanaka remained as the on-air host. A well-known and experienced media personality thanks to years of radio and television reporting, he was also a very dedicated and talented writer of fiction, with many stories published in *Bamboo Ridge* and elsewhere, and a very well-received collection of fiction, *In Good Company*, published by University of Hawai'i Press. His earnest yet laid back delivery held together pieces that were often extremely

Audience members line up outside HPR studios. Here, the Hacklers show off their bow ties for Father's Day show.

different in tone and content. In the studio and on the airwaves, then, Cedric was a constant for *Aloha Shorts*.

But our discussions also led to several significant modifications. We decided that as much as possible, the shows would be broadcast as recorded, which meant carefully selecting and organizing the pieces, then scripting the performances together into the twenty-nine minute format required for radio. The live audiences at the Atherton would therefore be hearing three shows in succession, with an intermission between shows two and three. Second, we would select themes to provide a rationale for why poems and stories were performed together. One theme—Women, for instance—usually informed all three shows taped in a single evening. But sometimes two themes would be featured, and one of our themes—Sex, Drugs, and Rock 'n' Roll—was a trinity: three in one, one in three.

Another crucial decision was to secure a house band. A familiar feature of many serial radio programs, such as *A Prairie Home Companion*, regular musical accompaniment would simplify the process of securing musicians for each taping, but more importantly, would also provide a comforting continuity from week to week. Our first choice was Hamajang, "Honolulu's favorite jugless jug band," with deep roots in the local music scene, and with a respected and irreverent wordsmith, former newspaper editor Derek Ferrar, playing a mean 'ukulele out front. Charley Myers (guitar, steel guitar, and vocals), Yash Wichmann-Walczak (accordion and a homemade washtub bass, known affectionately as the Yash-tub), and other invited guests made up the band, whose distinctive sound, amazing responsiveness to our ever-changing themes, and general goofiness became a hallmark of the *Aloha Shorts* studio experience. Derek and the band also came up with the *Aloha Shorts* theme song; you'll find the words elsewhere in this collection.

How we prepared the first shows soon became standard operating procedure. Months beforehand, we held brainstorming sessions for selecting themes. As longtime readers of *Bamboo Ridge* all three of us would then suggest possible poems or stories. To make sure we had considered all our options, after the meeting, Craig would also go through the entire Bamboo Ridge Press content database, searching for titles that suggested a piece might fit the theme.

After assembling a list of candidates, Craig turned to the complete run of Bamboo Ridge publications in his office (the Center for Biographical Research at the University of Hawaiʻi–Mānoa), and made photocopies of the pieces that proved suitable. At our next meeting, we decided which pieces seemed especially promising, and then set to work organizing them into individual shows.

Although a single piece occasionally took up an entire show, orchestrating a handful of offerings that explored different facets of the theme tended to work best. Because each show was confined to the strict twenty-nine-minute format, we soon developed a handy classification system for organizing the pieces. "Papa Bears" were complete short stories or sections from novels that would take ten minutes or longer to perform. You could usually only have one on each show. "Mama Bears" usually took five to seven minutes. They were shorter prose pieces, very substantial poems, or complete dramatic monologues. (Lee Cataluna's *Folks You Meet in Longs* proved to be a Mama Bear goldmine.) Two Mama Bears could accompany a Papa Bear, but the show would be tight. "Baby Bears" came in under three minutes. Almost always poems, two to four could be performed on a show, depending on the number of Mama Bears.

Only after the theme and the contents were set did we cast the shows. Because we had all been involved in Hawaiʻi's theater scene for many years, we knew many of the actors in town, and could usually agree on a first choice with some backups relatively quickly. For efficiency's sake, and particularly for scheduling rehearsals, an actor would usually perform two or three pieces during an evening taping.

Sammie invited and confirmed the actors, while Craig tracked down the writers for permission to perform their pieces. This often resembled detective work. Not surprisingly, for a poet whose sole contribution to *Bamboo Ridge* was published in 1979, the contact information was often no longer correct. Once Sammie had completed casting, she and Phyllis divided the actors up between them, and scheduled and directed rehearsals. Because we were careful when casting, and because we came to know which actors were talented and dependable voice performers, only two rehearsals were usually needed before the taping. For context, a Papa Bear usually required a total of four to six hours of rehearsal.

Long Papa Bears often had to be edited, and were often cut further in rehearsal. After working the pieces with the actors, Phyllis and Sammie provided Craig with more precise estimates of performance times, and he began to write those parts of the shows that Cedric would read as host. The scripting process was relatively formulaic.

The opening and closing were basically templates: introducing listeners to the show, listing the sponsors, and crediting the co-producers and production staff at the end. A description of each show's theme would follow the opening, and before each piece, a brief introduction would give the title and the author, relate the poem or story to the theme, provide some biographical information on the author, and identify the performer. Brief transitions linked the pieces together.

Running between thirty seconds and two minutes, these scripted sections took up between four to five minutes of each half-hour show. Craig circulated a draft of all three shows to Sammie and Phyllis a few days before the taping. Their suggestions were then incorporated into a final large print draft that went to Cedric. Copies were also prepared for the co-producers, and most importantly, for Jason, who would use the script as his guide when preparing the recorded shows for broadcast. Estimated times were listed for all sections; keeping "on time" in performance became everyone's concern.

Phyllis kept Hamajang and HPR in the loop on the selected show themes and provided the station with details of the authors and actors for publicity purposes or wrote the press releases. She also managed the *Aloha Shorts* emails and social media, as well as outreach into specific communities that might be particularly interested in the evening's subject matter.

At the Atherton Studio

The live recordings were held roughly once a month on Sunday nights, from 7:00 to 9:00 p.m. in HPR's intimate performance space at their Honolulu studios and offices. (Over the years we recorded two sets of shows elsewhere—at the Hawai'i Book and Music Festival at the Honolulu Civic Center, and on Maui at the Historic 'Iao Theater.) The co-producers and recording engineer Jason arrived early to set the lights, microphones, and any special features for that evening. Our house band, Hamajang, or guest musicians loaded in their instruments, did a sound check, and rehearsed some of their numbers. The actors came at 6:00 p.m. for their sound checks in the Studio. The audience started lining up outside HPR on Kāheka Street at 6:30 p.m., and the house opened at 6:45 p.m. Hamajang played three or four pieces before we began taping, and these selections often revealed that the band had gone to great lengths to come up with music that suited the theme—offbeat holiday music for a Christmas show, or on one memorable night devoted to science fiction, a performance of "The Time Warp" from *The Rocky Horror Picture Show*, complete with costumes and musical guests.

Right before taping started, Cedric would welcome everyone, explain how the evening would proceed, and urge the audience to respond as they would at any live performance—only louder. Then it was on with the scripted shows.

Sammie remained in the studio, monitoring the actors and taking photographs. Craig and Phyllis were in the control booth with Jason, their eyes fixed on the script and on copies of the pieces being performed, carefully noting slips and stumbles that would have to be re-recorded at the end of the evening. They were also comparing the estimated with the actual performance times, and if necessary, were already thinking about possible cuts. Assistant Producer Daniel Akiyama often helped out in the booth, and also worked with Sheryl Lynch, the house manager, at getting the audience in and out of the studio.

After the intermission, Hamajang would play three more songs, and then the final show would be taped. When the audience had left, Cedric and the actors would record patches for those sections that needed fixing. There usually weren't many. Later, Jason would edit the corrections into the final mix, cut the agreed-upon sections on the rare occasion that the show ran too long, and add incidental Hamajang music if it ran short.

These broadcast versions then went to Phyllis, who listened to them and offered further corrections or revisions, if needed. The three shows from a single taping would be broadcast in sequence a few months later, Tuesdays at 6:30 p.m., on what was at the time the station's news and entertainment channel, HPR-2. Reruns were broadcast during the summer, or at the appropriate time of year for shows with holiday themes—Halloween, Christmas, New Year's.

A word or two should be said about the taping atmosphere. HPR's regular on-air promotion and frequent Honolulu newspaper mentions, when combined with free admission and a capacity of only seventy-five in HPR's Atherton Studio, resulted in consistently full houses by our third or fourth taping. The audiences were not disappointed. Even when the theme or the pieces were light-hearted, everyone in the studio could feel the intensity of focus. The actors had been selected because they were good, and as each one performed, often brilliantly, a sense of healthy competition was rising in the others, creating a momentum and a heightened energy.

The *Aloha Shorts* producers also turned the tapings into events in themselves. For instance, we invited the audience to come in costume for our Halloween shows—which we recorded in July. For Father's Day, we requested the audience wear their favorite neckties. And when we showcased the fiction of Lisa Linn Kanae, we had audience members compete in a contest taken straight from one of her stories: to see who could inflate a condom fastest with Alka-Seltzer and a glass of water.

Aloha Shorts Halloween Costume Contest

Special promotions and community initiatives drew attention to the show, and attracted new performers and audiences. We announced open auditions for anyone who wanted to read on *Aloha Shorts*. Over seventy people showed up, and a few were actually cast. We also auditioned high school performers for a show about youth, and Phyllis and Sammie flew over early to Maui to audition and rehearse actors for a show taped there in Wailuku.

Though Hamajang was our stalwart house band, on certain shows we also featured special musical guests. Grammy-nominated pianist/violinist/singer-songwriter Barbara Higbie performed on one of our Women Writers evenings. The UH Filipino Rondalla led by Ricardo Trimillos played during our evening devoted to Pinoy literature of Hawai'i. Maui artists George Kahumoku, Jr. and Gail Swanson performed on the Maui No Ka 'Oi shows taped at the Historic 'Iao Theater in Wailuku. And Jon, Jamaica, and Duncan Osorio, with Tim Sprowls, were integral to the Hawaiian literature shows—one of the few times when the music was not incidental, but scripted into the broadcast.

A single actor at the microphone was the norm, but when dialogue was key to a piece, we would cast two actors. Lois-Ann Yamanaka's "Name Me Is" featured devastating performances by Donalyn Dela Cruz and James Kimo Bright. A two-part Christmas story featured several voices, and when the theme was Hawai'i plays, all the excerpts featured multiple actors. On occasion, separate pieces were woven together, the actors performing antiphonally. And rarely, but memorably, sound effects greatly enhanced some performances—most notably, perhaps, the voice of Pavarotti punctuating Stephanie Keiko Kong's outstanding reading of Lisa Linn Kanae's "Luciano and Da Break Room Divas." (Jason outdid himself that night.)

To many people's surprise, though, what you would not hear on *Aloha Shorts* was the voice of the poet or the fiction writer. There were exceptions. Although authors often attended the tapings to hear their work read—one writer flew in from the East Coast!—for our Readers' Choice shows we conceived of a special occasion when the authors would actually read their work. Happily, the authors selected by our listeners were all strong and effective readers, although Sammie and Phyllis still offered to help the writers prepare. (Elsewhere in this collection, Darrell Lum describes what this was like.)

When we recorded two shows in the Mission Memorial Auditorium for the Hawai'i Book and Music Festival

Devon Nekoba, Shiro Kawai, and Ann Brandman taping a two-part holiday special that aired in December 2009

celebrating the writing of Lee Cataluna, actors performed selections from her fiction and plays, but we asked Lee herself to read from her journalism. Because her newspaper columns were written from her point of view, we decided they should be heard in her voice.

Why did we not simply record the artists who had produced the work? One reason was the show's mission. As Cedric said every week, *Aloha Shorts* was a showcase for Hawai'i's writers, *and* its actors and musicians. We wanted audiences to hear just how talented Hawai'i's voice performers were, and as actors, writers, and directors ourselves, we were personally fascinated with how one artist presents the work of another in a different medium.

But to be entirely honest, most writers' work is simply more effective when an actor presents it. Admittedly, some poets and fiction writers have a strong dramatic sense, a fine ear, and a clear and effective speaking voice. In fact, on two occasions we cast authors to perform the work of someone else. When casting a poem written from a woman's perspective by Wing Tek Lum, we realized that fiction writer Lisa Linn Kanae would be the perfect choice, and Brenda Kwon's experience as a spoken word poet made her an excellent candidate for another piece. But many writers tend to see, rather than hear, their writing, so in virtually all cases, after selecting a poem, story, or play, we then asked the writer's permission for someone else to perform it.

As we became more ambitious over the years, we also extended the range of the pieces. Of course, with over thirty years of Bamboo Ridge material to choose from, we had literally thousands of options. Occasionally, though, a theme would jog a producer's memory, and up would come the perfect piece—but not one published by Bamboo Ridge Press. It could be a part of a play, a section from a Lois-Ann Yamanaka novel, or a poem or story that first appeared in another Hawai'i or Pacific journal or anthology.

Since the theme was always the thing, we did sometimes ask an author for permission to include the perfect piece. Our Pacific Writers evening provides perhaps the most notable example. Working with poets and critics Craig Santos Perez and Brandy McDougall as consultants, we followed our template in everything but the origin of the pieces. Had *Aloha Shorts* continued, we almost certainly would have extended further our boundaries of choice, while remaining committed to performing literature with special meaning for Hawai'i.

For everyone involved in *Aloha Shorts*, the most gratifying times were when people told us how much they valued the show. "When I was little, I loved being read to," one loyal audience member explained, "and now I have that again." Other listeners told us about driveway moments—sitting in the car, not being able to leave until the end of a story. One person described how she deliberately left her home forty-five minutes early for her Tuesday hula rehearsal, so she could listen to *Aloha Shorts* without distractions on the way. We also heard from teachers of Hawai'i literature, who were gratefully using the podcasts of the shows posted online by Bamboo Ridge. The full houses for every taping was another sign, and so were the people who called in during HPR pledge drives and explicitly said that they were contributing because of *Aloha Shorts*. Clearly, the show made many people feel that they were lucky to live Hawai'i.

Why Did the Show End, and What Was "From Me to You"?

The last *Aloha Shorts* taping took place on May 6, 2012; those shows were aired that summer. Hawai'i Public Radio then broadcast encore performances each week until March 26, 2013. Why did we stop?

The immediate cause was that Phyllis committed to directing a new play, and proposed taking a sabbatical. When we thought it over, however, we soon realized that none of us wanted to continue *Aloha Shorts* without the other two. Since we had produced 100 half-hour shows in three-and-a-half years, we therefore decided to resign together, while still proud of the results. We had enjoyed our collaboration so much over the years, however, that when offered the opportunity, we reassembled to produce two more quite different shows. Jason Taglianetti, our recording engineer, had created a program called *Applause in a Small Room* that recorded performances before a live audience in the Atherton Studio for later broadcast on HPR. Since that is what we had been doing, and since many listeners were telling HPR that they missed *Aloha Shorts*, we agreed to create two one-hour shows for taping on Saturday, September 13, 2014. This time there actually was an admission fee, but we sold out quickly again, so we added a Friday night taping as well. This gave us the luxury of two versions for editing purposes. These shows were broadcast as episodes of *Applause in a Small Room* on May 3 and 10, 2015.

Entitled "From Me to You," the result both was and was not an *Aloha Shorts* reboot. Recalling our Hawaiian Literature shows, we decided to integrate the literature, music, and commentary seamlessly. To this end, we invited Jon Osorio, the featured musician on those Hawaiian shows, to perform the music, and to serve as host. The theme was also a departure. Instead of a topic, we chose a mode of address. All the featured poetry, fiction, and songs had to be addressed to a "you," often by a vividly dramatic "I." Studio and radio audiences could then choose to identify with the "you," or not.

All the pieces were linked to Hawai'i, and many had first appeared in *Bamboo Ridge*, whose editors gave us permission to perform the work, as did the authors, who received royalties because of the admission charge. Though the shows were not called *Aloha Shorts*, because they represent our last collaboration as producers, and because they strongly depended on our relationship with Bamboo Ridge Press, we have featured "From Me to You" as one of the theme clusters in this anthology.

Suggestions for Use

Like *Aloha Shorts*, this collection brings disparate materials together into a coherent and interesting whole. At the heart of both enterprises are the pieces themselves. Some from the late 1970s, others very recent, the poems, fiction, and other modes of writing gathered here are printed in full, as they first appeared in Bamboo Ridge Press publications. For our purposes, what they have in common is that they were all performed for broadcast on Hawai'i Public Radio. A single click on **www.bestofalohashorts.com**, will take readers to audio files of the readings of the poems and stories included here and performed on *Aloha Shorts*.

A question that arose in the editing was how we would deal with the issue of diacritical marks on Hawaiian words. Because *Bamboo Ridge* has been appearing for forty years, the poetry and fiction we selected often follow the protocols of different periods during this longstanding editorial debate. Rather than setting a 2018 policy that would then be imposed on all the contents, we decided to give readers the texts as first presented to the world. In some cases, the authors have insisted on this; in others, retaining the original spelling actually contributes to the feeling that the poem or story is of another time.

In addition to this Introduction, brief comments by actors and writers involved in *Aloha Shorts* appear throughout the collection—sometimes offering insight into a particular piece, sometimes responding more generally to the experience. We have also solicited comments from other stakeholders in the show—the sponsors, the musicians, the host. Together, they offer glimpses into what it was like to be part of *Aloha Shorts*.

Some of the poems and stories are clustered together because they were performed together, showing how our themes set up interesting contrasts and affinities between very different works. Some pieces are grouped under themes created while editing this collection, although the primary reason why all of them are here is because of the quality of the work, and the special magic brought to it by its performance.

The result is an anthology of some of the finest poetry and prose produced by Hawai'i's writers, appearing once more in the publication that was their first home, with the added value of a link to the audio archive of thought-provoking, stirring, and highly enjoyable performances that delivered this writing to listeners throughout Hawai'i each week, on *Aloha Shorts*.

Hamajang Calls
Derek Ferrar
musician

Every band dreams of driving down the road and hearing themselves come on the radio. For us Hamajang guys, *Aloha Shorts* made the dream come true every week.

True to our band motto, SNAFK—or, Situation Normal, All Funny Kine—we lucked/stumbled into our run as the *Aloha Shorts* house band, which held so many career highlights for us: the intimate acoustics of the Atherton Studio, for starters, and the rapt attention of each month's live audience, often stacked with local luminaries. It could be nerve-wracking, though, since every live goof was immortalized on tape.

Challenged by the production dream team to match our music to each show's literary theme, we got to stretch our creative sinews some. (OK, maybe a little too far at times, but hey, that's Hamajang.) When we were asked to compose a theme song, I couldn't fight the urge to pun, and spent long hours on Wikipedia hunting for writers with notable sartorial quirks. I wish I could have worked in local authors too, but I wasn't really sure where to go with that beyond Darrell Lum's "Beer Can Hat."

It stung when the show ended, but we did come away with a stash of recordings—mahalo to ace engineer Jason Taglianetti—that we dubbed *Hamajang Calls*, in honor of our timeless radio experience. Thanks to those discs, us guys and a couple dozen assorted victims get to relive our *Aloha Shorts* glory days over and over again, forevers.

HamajangBand.com

*Hamajang, the *Aloha Shorts* house band, was Derek Ferrar ('ukulele, cajon, voice), Charley Myers (guitar, steel guitar, voice), Yash Wichmann-Walczak (accordion, washtub bass), and Mark Scrufari (guitar).

Aloha Shorts Theme Song

Shakespeare in his fancy ruffles, Chaucer in his tights
Basho in his old kimono, Tom Wolfe in his whites
Plenny great writers, throughout all time
Have labored hard at looking fine
But you are simply too divine
In your Aloha Shorts
Oh, your sharp Aloha Shorts

Homer's got his party toga, Tolstoy's got his beard
Mark Twain's got that wild style, Capote's just plain weird
Great men of letters, from A to Zed
Have rhapsodized about their threads
But you could really knock 'em dead
With your Aloha Shorts
Oh, your cool Aloha Shorts

Rumi in his funky turban, Tagore wrapped his shawl
Toni Morrison with her natty cornrows, Vic Hugo wearin' nothing at all
Lao Tzu's whiskers, Fitzgerald's spats
Dickinson's frock, Zora Hurston's hats
Hey you could show 'em where it's at
In your Aloha Shorts
Yeah, your hot Aloha Shorts

Chekhov's glasses, Kesey's dyes
Neruda's caps, Saul Bellow's ties
Well, you could take the Nobel Prize
In your Aloha Shorts
Your chic Aloha Shorts,
Oh those loud Aloha Shorts
Oh those boss . . . Aloha . . . Shorts!

*Words & Music by Derek Ferrar © 2009
Performed by Hamajang

New Year's Eve 1991
Mavis Hara
from *An Offering of Rice*, first aired January 6, 2009

At a temple in Tachikawa, the night is cold but no wind nips at fingers, face, and ears. We are with friends, other *sansei* from Hawai'i. Uncomfortable, don't know if we really should be here, we are outsiders after all, not really Japanese.

Twelve o'clock:

We enter the temple courtyard through the unpainted wooden gate, walk along the path between cedar trees so tall they must have tasted the same rain as my grandfather, one hundred years ago, when he lived in Japan. A priest standing on the raised platform beside the great temple bell chants a sutra to greet the New Year. His slow syllables float above us as we walk toward him to the center of the courtyard with its bonfire of giant wood beams. A small crowd of Japanese families, the temple's congregation, surrounds the fire; they open their circle and let us in. Their wool coats smell of camphor and incense. The cold of the last midnight of December is at our backs; the orange glow of the fire warms our faces and chests. The night is still. The fire is gentle, flames bloom off the timbers like flowers. Sparks from the tips of the burning logs break off and scatter, rising. Orange sparks that trace commas through the cold gray charcoal air. Hundreds, thousands of chrysanthemum petal sparks. Each is the shape the Japanese give to the soul. Separating, they rise together in a crowd, in a column six feet around. Slow as the sutra being chanted, they float upward. The fire continues burning gently and one group of sparks replaces another. They rise higher and higher, each one still glowing, into the darkness above the tops of the cedar trees.

The black-robed priest pulls the red-and-white silk cords attached to a wooden beam hanging in front of the giant temple bell. Red, the color of blood; white, the color of ashes. One pull, two, three, the beam swings faster and faster, in an arc, a comma, a curve, until wood striking iron booms out round and resonant, the voice of the Buddha, no beginning, no end. Our group in the courtyard exhales in wonder. Our breath is pulled into the river of sparks and rises with them to the treetops. At the priest's invitation, the worshippers

Kat Koshi reads "New Year's Eve 1991"

begin a single-file procession up the platform stairs. We each bow and take the red-and-white silk cords in hand. We pull wood toward iron. The bell sounds again and again. Concentric rings of sound encircle the bonfire, the people, the giant cedar trees. Each peal rises with the sparks and is replaced by the next, rising higher and higher, carving a warm tunnel of sound, reaching toward heaven.

STORIES

As the *Aloha Shorts* editors combed through the *Bamboo Ridge* archives for pieces that fit each show's chosen theme, we often stopped dead in our foraging to read the stories we encountered. Just as our listeners talked about their driveway moments—when you just *have* to stay in your car to hear the end of a story, even if the three cartons of Ben & Jerry's are softening in the back seat—certain pieces caught us and wouldn't let go. That was telling—we knew then that we should pay particular attention to those discoveries.

The stories we've gathered here reveal the intimacy beneath mundane relationships, as with the mother, daughter, and granddaughter in Nora Okja Keller's "Rockhead"; let us laugh at the hapless reality of a defiant new bachelor in Cedric Yamanaka's "Benny's Bachelor Cuisine"; and give us simple truths about love and friendship in Darrell H.Y. Lum's classic story of Bobo and "Da Beer Can Hat." These are three of the best.

Paris Priore-Kim
performer

For as long as I can remember, my interest has always been piqued by the notes of foreign accents and languages. As a very young child, I remember contorting the muscles in my face to sing "Supercalifragilisticexpialidocious" in order to sound like Julie Andrews. Subsequently, I attended school in Switzerland, and out of necessity was compelled to understand the mechanics of speaking Swiss French, but also those of sounding Swiss French, in order to fit in as an adolescent.

The mechanics of pronunciation are fascinating and complex. Most people say that you need a "good ear," when in fact you need both an ear and a mirror. In my efforts to reproduce the sounds I hear, I find that they derive from the position of the tongue, the shape of the lips, the placement of the jaw, the amount of aspiration—just to name a few of the factors.

I welcomed the work of producing Asian accents for my *Aloha Shorts* readings, but identifying the sounds of consonants, vowels, and diphthongs in Korean was new territory and laden with responsibility. I feel a duty to do this work with respect, and looking back I will always find spots that could be improved with the discipline of closer study and practice—and a good mirror.

Rockhead
Nora Okja Keller
from *Bamboo Ridge* Issue #75, first aired February 8, 2011

My baby's head is so round—round as a rare and perfect piece of obsidian found on Waimānalo Beach, polished instead of flattened or fractured, by the force of water.

I love her round-headed perfection, my daughter's head shape so like mine, and my mother's when she was a child.

While I was growing up, my mother would study her daughters for signs of herself, then make pronouncements binding us to her and our fates. To oldest sister, she would say: Our hair is like seaweed, so black and slick it can never hold a comb; Watch that you don't fly away. To second sister, she'd say: You've got my dimples; Life has to pinch your cheeks hard to make you happy.

My mother would tell third sister to hold out her hands, fingers pressed tightly together. See, she would sigh, see how the light shines through the cracks? Like me, you'll have trouble holding onto what you most want.

When she would look at me as if she was seeing both me and a memory, I knew what would come out of her mouth: Rockhead. Just like me, she'd say, shaking her head. You'll have a hard life, always banging against the current. Worse than a boy, more stubborn than a stone.

But she would say these things with pride so I would know that she loved me.

And every time she called me Rockhead, I'd ask her, "why? how come? how do you know? what does it mean?" pestering her for a story, hoping to learn more about my mother and, in turn, about the secrets of myself.

At night, when my mother unwound her hair, combing through the heavy silk with her fingers, I'd press against her, close as she would let me, and wait. If I was lucky, she would notice me. Baby Girl, she might say, pick out my white hairs. Or Youngest Daughter, massage my temples.

I'd sit cross-legged on the floor and wait for my mother to lie down and slip her head into my lap. I'd stroke her forehead, the sides of her face, the top of her head where the spirit escapes at night. When she'd begin to tell her story, I'd part her hair into sections, using my nails to find and pluck the white strands. As she talked, I'd stick the oily roots onto a sheet of one of the underground papers, either the *Korean Independence* or the *Student Revolutionary*, that found its way into our village outside of Pusan. And after the story, after my mother fell asleep, I'd crumple the paper into a ball and burn it in the flues that warmed the underbelly of our home. As I drifted off to sleep, breathing in the scent of hair and smoke, I'd imagine that words wrapped in my mother's hair drifted into our dreams and spiraled up to heaven.

I am still trying to find order in the stories my mother doled out in bits and pieces, in the hopes that in doing so I can find significance and sanity in my own life. And so that I can warn my daughter, and protect her. Because what I remember most strongly from my mother's storytelling is not something that she told me, but something that I felt: her head was no longer round.

My mother was told that the most famous fortuneteller in Seoul, paid to read her head at birth, said that she was the most round-headed baby she had ever seen. In a round-headed family that valued head shape along with money and auspicious birth charts, this was the highest praise.

The fortuneteller predicted that because of her roundness, because of the class she was born into, and because of the sign she was born under, my mother would be very spoiled and very happy. Everything would roll her way.

This was true for perhaps the first seven years of her life.

My favorite fairy tales when I was growing up were my mother's own baby-time stories. When we played make-pretend, my sisters and I pretended to be our mother, whose early days were filled with parties in Seoul and candy and fancy Western dresses. I pictured most of the things she told us about by finding something in my own life to compare it to and thinking, same thing only one thousand times better. When she told us about a doll from France with blue eyes painted in a porcelain face, I took my own pine and rag doll, put a cup over her head and imagined a toy a thousand times better.

The one thing my mother talked about that neither my sisters nor I could imagine or comprehend was ice cream. We just had no reference for it in our own lives, and when we'd push our mother for a definition, her descriptions left us even more dubious and mystified.

It's like sucking on an ice cold, perfectly ripe peach, my mother once tried to explain.

Then why not just eat a peach, we asked.

Because it's not the same, my mother said. That's just what it feels like in your mouth. It feels like a ripe peach and like the snow, and like how a cloud full of rain must feel if you could bite into it.

I remember biting into my own honey and nut candy that my mother made for us during the harvest and watching her talk. She would shut her eyes, but I could still see them move back and forth, back and forth under their lids. She seemed very magical, like a princess from heaven, when she talked about ice cream.

When I married my GI and came to Hawai'i, I was surprised to see how common and how cheap ice cream was. Once I found out what it was, I bought a carton of each flavor I could find—cherry vanilla, strawberry, banana, pistachio, Neapolitan, chocolate chip, macadamia nut. We'd have ice cream every night after dinner. At first my husband encouraged me, glad that I was becoming American. But then he found out that I was also eating ice cream for lunch and for breakfast. And that I cried after eating a bowl of a particularly good flavor because it reminded me that when my mother was a round-headed child princess, she took a bite out of heaven.

After he found out these things, my husband put me on a diet.

I try to maintain my baby's round head. I make sure her hats and headbands aren't too tight. When I shampoo her hair, I am careful that I don't use too much pressure and leave unintentional dents. I make sure she sleeps on her stomach so her skull won't flatten out in the back, and I maintain a constant vigilance, checking on her throughout the night so that I can catch her when she flips over. This is hard work, and I do it in secret because I do not want to hear my husband talk about god and genetics. I know better because of my mother, than to think that head shape is fixed for life.

In the years before her head changed, my mother's father was a middle school official. He was the one who gave my mother her doll from France, fancy dresses, a taste for ice cream. He was also the one who taught her lessons, drilling her in math and history. Because of him, my mother wanted to be the best girl student in the primary school.

"I studied, studied, studied," my mother would say, "so I could be the best. But every time we took the tests, I always placed second. Number one was always my best friend, who I hated at that time of year."

"Every year," she said, "I wished to be number one. One year, though, I figured out that my wishing wasn't enough to make it happen, because my best friend was also wishing to be number one. Her wish was blocking my wish. So that year, when it came time to write our wishes on the paper we would burn and send to heaven, I told my best friend she should wish to be the prettiest girl, since she was already the smartest. When she said okay and I saw her write this down, I snuck away and wrote on my own paper, I wish to be number one in school."

My mother would always become sad at this point in the story, and when my sisters and I asked if she got her wish, she'd always say, "Yes, and I'm sorry."

The year my mother's wish came true was the year Japan invaded Korea. The year her father and his colleagues were taken away. The year that her best friend had to drop out of school because her family could not afford to pay the education fee demanded by the New Japanese Provisional Government.

My mother had to learn a new alphabet, and new words for everyday things. She had to learn to answer to a new name, to think of herself and her world in a new way. To hide her secret self.

These are the things my mother taught me, and these are the things that have enabled me to survive in this new country. Because of my mother's early lessons, I can eat crackseed without making a face or spitting. I can look up at the shopboy at Woolworth who says "Watcha like, lady?" and hide my fear. And I can smile when everyone talks too fast with words that make no sense, when all I really want to do is scream and scream and never stop.

This is the way my mother also survived, but she paid a price. I think this, the way my mother hid herself, the way her lived life deviated from the person she was born to be, is what changed the shape of her head.

In Korea, the elders warned those of us haunting the American PX for work or handouts about mixing our blood with the foreigners. Though nothing specific was said, my girlfriends and I imagined that big-nose, blue-and-blind-eyed monsters would sprout from out wombs if we mated with the Americans. Still, that did not stop us from going where the money and food was. I know I was willing to risk anything because I was hungry, even marrying a foreigner and leaving my home country.

When I became pregnant, I could not help worrying about what my baby would look like, wonder if she would be a monster or a human. Korean or Other. Me or not me. Even walking the streets of Honolulu, seeing for my own eyes the normal-looking "chop suey" children, I could not stifle the voices of the village elders whispering, "Monsters, monsters."

Now, as I look at my daughter, I do not know how I could have doubted her perfection. Her hair is reddish brown, not black, her eyes, though brown, are cut differently than mine. But her head is round.

I cup her tiny head in my palms and whisper, "I am so proud of you. You are a rockhead like your mother and your mother's mother. Only a thousand times better."

Benny's Bachelor Cuisine
Cedric Yamanaka
from *The Best of HONOLULU Fiction*, first aired February 3, 2009

Benny Akina and Denise Park met at a New Year's Eve cocktail party thrown at the luxurious Diamond Head beach house of Jules Reinnard. Monsieur Reinnard, of course, is the famous owner of Waikīkī's Silver Oyster Pub and Café. Benny Akina was a restaurant critic for *The Honolulu Advertiser*. Denise Park, one of Hawai'i's most respected chefs. Over spinach salads, crab cakes, fresh oysters, and rigatoni, they talked about the weather, politics, sports, and—the subject they shared the highest mutual interest—food. Great banquets, unforgettable dishes, secret recipes, and favorite restaurants.

A year later—after dozens of dinner dates and home-cooked meals—Benny Akina and Denise Park were married. Together, they were a happy couple. Gifted with looks, intelligence, grace, style, success, and youth. Life was as sweet and smooth as a perfect cabernet.

Three years later, they bought the Silver Oyster Pub and Café in Waikīkī. Jules Reinnard—after fifty-nine years in the restaurant business—retired. Benny handled the administrative affairs. Denise created amazing dishes in the kitchen. Lines formed outside the restaurant. The guest list included kings and queens, presidents, Hollywood stars, and champion athletes.

Two years later, Benny Akina and Denise Park finalized their divorce. Denise hired the finest attorney in town and got the houses, the cars, and the Silver Oyster Pub and Café. Benny got the shaft.

What had happened to this promising marriage? Benny asked himself the question hundreds of times.

Their union seemed to have been filled with love, respect, friendship. Denise always kept the house neat, made sure Benny's clothes were clean and pressed, prepared delicious meals. Benny brought home chocolates and dozens of long-stemmed roses, took Denise on long drives around the island on Sunday afternoons, politely endured the opera on public television with her—even though he wanted to watch Monday Night Football.

Perhaps, Benny thought, he was just not cut out for marriage. Had never been. He was a natural bachelor. And basically a slob. Leaving his bed unmade in the morning because at night, the sheets just got mixed up again. Leaving clothes on the floor because a shirt on a carpet was easier to find than one hanging in, say, a dark closet. Leaving his hairbrush uncleaned for years until it resembled a sea anemone because hair just needed to be combed again and brushes, well, they just got dirty again.

Dave Lancaster reads "Benny's Bachelor Cuisine"

Denise, on the other hand, was the opposite. She was a woman who liked neatness, order, and organization. Everything had its place. She arranged pots in her cupboard by size. Placed spices in alphabetical order. Made sure the television remote control was exactly perpendicular to the television set.

Maybe, thought Benny, little by little, it was these tiny differences that had disintegrated the real love Benny and Denise had shared. Like waves breaking on rocks, turning them gradually into sand.

One day—destitute and near penniless—Benny Akina walked down Beretania Street and came upon an empty shop with a "For Lease" sign taped to the window. That's when the idea hit him. A voice in the wind told him to open up a restaurant. A restaurant solely for bachelors. There must be millions of them out there, thought Benny. A place to make them feel at home. Or a place for married men to go so they, too—even for just a meal—could feel like a bachelor once again.

"What used to be here?" said Benny to the Realtor.

"A dress shop," the Realtor said.

"It's perfect," said Benny Akina. "I'll take it."

Thus Benny's Bachelor Cuisine was created. The menu was enough to bring a tear to any bachelor's eye. Spam and rice. Campbell's Soup. Instant saimin. An assortment of TV dinners. Bologna sandwiches. Vienna sausage. Pretzels. Pork and beans, with the option to eat them straight out of the can.

And the décor. Pure bachelor gems. Laundry baskets. A weight bench. Ashtrays with coins and car keys inside. Various athletic equipment. Magazines like *Sports Illustrated*, *Popular Mechanics*, *Esquire*, an occasional *Playboy*. Black velvet glow-in-the-dark posters of panthers, dragsters, Elvis, and Bruce Lee hung on the walls.

On its first day of business, Benny's Bachelor Cuisine received no guests. Not a soul. The second day was no different. Alas, neither was the third day. Benny began wondering if he had made a terrible mistake. On the fourth day, a young man wearing a silk shirt, Angels Flight pants, and Famolare shoes walked into the restaurant. He had perfect, blow-dried hair. A gold tear drop around his neck. Benny thought he was seeing a ghost from the seventies.

"You look familiar," said Benny.

"You might have seen me in the movies," the ghost from the seventies said, sitting down at table five. "I was in *Saturday Night Fever* . . . "

"Of course," said Benny. "I should have known . . . "

"Remember when John Travolta wins the disco dance contest? I'm in the background, watching him do this thing. Second guy from the left . . . "

The ghost from the seventies became the first official customer of Benny's Bachelor Cuisine when he ordered spaghetti with Ragu sauce. It was on the house.

Soon, word of mouth spread and Benny's Bachelor Cuisine flourished. Bachelors began gathering by the dozens. There were the young downtown professionals. Accountants, architects, and attorneys. Eating dinner before attacking Restaurant Row or Ward Centre. Thinking they ruled the world. Then there were the working class guys. Construction workers, stevedores, bus drivers. Enjoying a beer before heading off to a night of Hawaiian music. And then there were the older customers. Like the balding, sixty-year-old doctor who wished more than anything he was a bachelor again. While his wife was at the symphony, he was driving his red BMW convertible up and down Ke'eaumoku Street, looking for the perfect Korean bar.

"What's the secret to the success of Benny's Bachelor Cuisine?" a curious bachelor asked one day.

"I'm not quite sure," said Benny. "All I know is there's a lot of bachelors out there who are lonely. They need a place to go, a place to meet. And bachelors do get hungry . . . "

"But let's face it," the curious bachelor said, looking at his plate of canned chili. "The food here is kinda terrible . . . "

"That's part of the charm, I think. If folks want good food, they can go to thousands of other restaurants . . . "

Benny did it all. He bought the ingredients, prepared the food, served it, cleared the tables, washed dishes. Sometimes, he even played the role of psychiatrist. Take for example, the case of the gloomy account executive who thought he'd never find a girl.

"Girls don't like me," the account executive said, staring despondently at his plate of canned sardines. "I'm too dorky . . . "

"You'll find a girl," Benny said. "In the meantime, enjoy the freedom of your bachelorhood. Think of it like, uh, like you're a caterpillar . . . "

"Caterpillars are worms, aren't they?"

"Have patience," said Benny. "And before you know it, you'll find the girl of your dreams and your life will be transformed. Like a caterpillar turning into a beautiful butterfly . . . "

"Bachelors are worms, huh?"

Sometimes, Benny performed the duty of social worker. Here is the dilemma of Ray, a fireman.

"I lost my girl," said Ray. "My life is over."

"Don't talk like that," said Benny. "There'll be others."

"Not like Suzanne," said Ray, a tear falling into his bowl of canned chunky stew.

"Sure there'll be," said Benny. "Trust me. I was married once . . . "

Yes, bachelors gathered at Benny's Bachelor Cuisine and talked of fish that got away, waves that had been surfed, cars, deals, beers that had been drunk, and—of course—women.

"There's a girl with the best set of legs at work," said one bachelor. "When she uses the Xerox machine, I wait patiently behind her and tell her to take her time . . . "

"There are way too many wahines calling me up," complained another bachelor. "I can't get any sleep. As soon as I lie down, the phone rings . . . "

"Listen to us," one brave bachelor finally said, standing up. "We sound like a bunch of kids in a high school locker room. Treating women like objects. Aren't you fellas ashamed of yourselves? Don't you all wanna get married? Have kids? Take on responsibility? Share your life with someone? Experience true love?"

The poor soul was booed louder than a BYU touchdown at Aloha Stadium.

As for Benny, he returned to the lifestyle he had once thrived upon before his unfortunate marriage. Sitting around the laundromat with other bachelors. Playing poker until the wee hours of the morning. Drinking a dozen different liquors in a dozen different places with a dozen different girls. Laughing, joking. While other less fortunate bachelors stood around dance floors like those statues on Easter Island, Benny Akina was the king of parties.

Secretly, though—very secretly—Benny often thought about Denise. Not only did he miss her venison, her rabbit, her soufflés. He missed her. Her smile, her warmth, the way she filled an otherwise empty house.

One day—one magical day—the unthinkable occurred. The afternoon began like any other, feeding hungry bachelors.

"I'll have the hot dogs," a customer in Levi's jeans said. "Three of them."

"Hot or cold?" said Benny.

"Don't ask stupid questions," the somewhat belligerent bachelor said. "Cold, of course. Right out of the refrigerator. How else do real bachelors eat hot dogs?"

"What's your special today?" another bachelor asked.

"We have a potato chip and beer combo," said Benny, somewhat proudly. After all, he had come up with the dish himself.

"Potato chips?" the discriminating bachelor said, rather disappointed. "That seems so, I don't know, boring . . . "

"Boring?" said Benny. "You call seventeen different kinds of potato chips boring?"

"Seventeen? No way. Get out of here . . . "

"Sour cream and onion, barbecue, cool ranch, extra crispy, low salt . . . "

All of a sudden—for the first time ever—a woman walked into Benny's Bachelor Cuisine. Jaws dropped. The insurance men turned off their calculators. Two crane operators stopped comparing tattoos. Dead silence. It was Denise Park.

"W-what are you doing here?" said Benny, not realizing he was walking backwards, moving away from Denise as if she was Frankenstein's monster.

"I'm hungry," said Denise, with a meek smile. "This is a restaurant. I'd like to order something to eat."

"C-can't you read the sign outside?" said Benny. "It says Benny's Bachelor Cuisine. You know what a b-bachelor is?"

"So?" said Denise. "Women can eat cold hot dogs and Spam and rice." She studied the menu. "The eggs simmered in Tabasco sauce sounding interesting. But let me give you a little tip. People are becoming a bit more health conscious. You should turn towards lighter, more healthier foods. That's what we're doing at the Silver Oyster Pub and Café. One of our most popular dishes is a linguine with asparagus and eggplant . . . "

"I'll have you know, Miss Smarty Pants, that our vegetarian special is one of our most popular selections. Kim chee and rice. Dill pickle on the side . . . "

"May I sit down?" said Denise.

"Jeez," said Benny, throwing his hands up to the ceiling in despair. "Yeah. Sure. Go ahead."

"Thank you," said Denise, selecting table four. A popular window seat with a view of the health club across the street. Bachelors fought like rabid dogs to sit there and watch the aerobics instructors going home from work. "I think . . . " said Denise. I think I'll have the Benny's Bachelor Cuisine Blue Plate Special. Cold, two-day old frozen pizza."

"Excellent choice," said stockbroker Hank.

"What did you really come here for?" said Benny.

"What do you mean?" said Denise.

"You didn't come here to eat two-day old pizza . . . "

"Doesn't the aging process bring out the flavor of the cheese?"

"Denise?"

"All right," said Denise, taking a deep breath. "I was worried about you. I missed you and I wanted to see you. Okay? Is there anything wrong with that?"

"I've missed you, too," said Benny.

"Oh, Benny," said Denise. "I miss rinsing your hair from the bathroom sink after you shave. I miss the way you squeeze toothpaste from the top of the tube, not the bottom. I miss the way you perspire after working out and still insist on lying on the couch without taking a shower . . . "

"I've missed you, too," said Benny. "I miss the way you always complain about me leaving the toilet seat up. The way you arrange your CDs in alphabetical order. The way you insist on wiping your silverware before eating with it . . . "

"Why did it fall apart?" said Denise.

"Maybe it's true what they say," said Benny. "Everything that's created is destined to fall apart."

"You think there's a chance that we could, uh, we could try again?" said Denise.

"Anything's possible," said Benny.

"Do you want to?" said Denise.

"Yes," said Benny. Then, "But what will happen to Benny's Bachelor Cuisine?"

"Leave it open," said Denise.

"Really?"

"Of course," said Denise. "There are a lot of bachelors out there who need a place to go to. A place to talk, share their triumphs, their sorrows . . . "

"I love you Denise," said Benny.

"I love you, Benny."

And to this day, Benny Akina and Denise Park are together. Living in a three-bedroom house in 'Āina Haina. Monday to Saturday, they work at their respective restaurants. Sundays, they spend together. Denise prepares a breakfast of waffles, eggs Benedict, and iced coffee. Like thousands of couples here in Hawai'i, they may go to the movies, spend the day at the beach, or stay at home with their two children.

Of course, there are still arguments every now and then. About Benny leaving crumbs in the carpet or dripping water on the bathroom floor after a shower. About Denise having to make sure the clocks in the house match the time given by the recording on the telephone. But both Benny Akina and Denise Park have learned that the love they have rediscovered is a precious gift that cannot be taken lightly, that these differences in personalities are what make the world go around.

Yes, even for bachelors.

Darrell H.Y. Lum
writer and performer

Hearing one's work read by someone else is always a little disconcerting. It sounds "wrong"; never is as it sounds in your own head. Going from the printed page to the radio waves really transforms the work into a new piece of literature *and* performance. And that's where the magic takes place. Just as the author tells the story solely through the printed page, the actors in *Aloha Shorts* have only their voices.

I've read "Da Beer Can Hat" countless times (and have enjoyed other actors performing it, most notably James Grant Benton, Jo Diotalevi, and UH Lab School speech students), and frankly, I've never thought about the story solely as an aural experience. After all, even with the *Aloha Shorts* tapings, the actors read before a live audience, and we have the pleasure of watching their facial expressions and gestures.

When asked to read my own story, and offered the chance to have co-producer Sammie Choy rehearse with me, I jumped at the opportunity. We spent an afternoon going over the story: she patiently advising me to emphasize a word here, make a change in voice there. I noted all her comments in the margins and tried again . . . and again. I could tell by her face that I wasn't hitting all the marks—maybe not any of them—as I realized that the actor has to control his or her voice to convey meaning without the radio audience being able to refer to the printed page, or being able to view facial expressions. Their reading from rehearsal through performance had to be consistent and replicable—much like a scientist having to prove a result was not a fluke.

People told me that when the lights were on and the tape was rolling, I did fine. But I didn't feel like a great scientist, or even a good voice actor. How do they make it sound so easy, so effortless?

I hope readers will take the time to listen to all the performances of the pieces in this collection, and like me, to marvel at the actors' abilities to make the stories their own.

Da Beer Can Hat

Darrell H.Y. Lum

from *Sun: Short Stories and Drama*, first aired May 25, 2010

I

You know, Bobo stay lolo in da head. Mental, you know. But he good fun sell newspaper and he smart fo' go by da cars when get stop light and sell to ladies, old ladies . . . and to da mokes who tell stink kine stuff about he belong in Kaneohe Hospital la' dat but in da end dey buy newspaypah and tip too! Most times dey give quartah and tell, "Keep da change," but sometimes dey give more.

Bobo he smart fo' time 'em good, him. He take long time get change fo' quartah at red light, bumbye da light change green and da guy tell, "Ay, ass okay, keep 'em," and step da gas. Bobo smile big and tell, "Tanks, eh." He time 'em real good. Me, everytime I get da real chang-kine guys and ho-man dey wait 'til da light turn red again fo' get dey ten cents change.

Coming-home-from-work time is da bes' time. I go after school sell papers wit' Bobo—supposed to go straight after—but I stay fool around school little while 'cuz Bobo always stay dere and watch my papers fo' me. Mistah Carvalho, mah district manager, get piss off but he no can do nutting, nobody like work fo' him already. He get smart wit' me I would tell 'em, "Ay, no make la' dat. I know one time you went dump all da inserts inside one big garbage can 'cause was late and nobody came fo' help put 'em inside da home deliveries." Ass what I would tell 'em. Yeah, you know.

One time I went ask Bobo what he do during da daytime when I go school. He tell he go by da supermarket and wheel da cart around. Used to be he wheel 'em around inside da store but da manager tell him no can, so he wheel 'em around outside in da parking lot.

I ask him what he saving up fo' and he tell, "One Motobecane, jes' like motorcycle dat. Tired pump my bike." Bobo's bike stay all junky, old style gooseneck and one-speed and one old newspaper bag hanging on da handlebars. Was shetty.

Me, I saving up for one skateboard, Cobra kine with heavy duty trucks, and one college edja-kay-shen. Ass what my fahdah tell me.

So me and Bobo, we stay together pretty good. Plenny guys tell, why I stay wit' Bobo. Dey tell he talk crooked, his mouth funny kine and sometimes drool lil' bit. I tell, "Watch out bra—he know kung fu and make like da wrestlah, da Missing Link, 'Whoaaa . . . yeah!'" But I went show him how fo' wipe his mout' before he sell newspaper to da custamah. I went buy him hanka-chief too. I wanted da kine wit' initials on top, "B.B." for Bobo. But I couldn't find, so I went buy one with "W" I tink, at sidewalk sale. Make 'em feel good, boy—I feel good too, though. He learn good, wipe his mouth first before he go to da customer. He no talk too good. Everytime guys tell, "Hah? What you talking, stupid." He only can try his best but no come out clear, "Heef-teen sants, pay-pah." But me, I used-to to it already.

Chee, one time one guy went run over his toes. Good ting he strong, boy. My fahdah said good ting he was wearing his rubber shoes, stay all had-it but it save his toes or maybe da guy went go so fast that never have time fo' smash his feet. But Bobo never tell nothing jes' like no sore, but must've been, yeah? One time he go show off, he tell, "I show you one trick," and he go poke one safety pin through his skin, you know da thick part by da thumb? Suckin' weird looking, safety pin through his thumb skin and him smiling up wit' his bolo-head. My fahdah said dat his fahdah no like him already and like throw him out of da house but da social worker say no can. Bobo no tell nothing about his fahdah but my fahdah tell, "Ass why he bolo-head everytime. Da fahdah no like when he bring home little bit money, he tink Bobo spend 'em or lose 'em on da way home so he give Bobo lickin's and shave his head." Ass why I ask my muddah fo' make him one, da kine, beer can hat. I go ask Bobo what his favorite team and he say, "Mah-keen-lee Tikahs." So I tell my muddah, "Can make 'em yellow and black? . . . For McKinley Tigers?" Tough man, da way my muddah can make 'em. She fast wit' da needles for knit. My fahdah laugh and tell, "I help. I help you Mama. I drink four beers right now so you can have da empty cans fo' make hat."

"Here Junior," he tell me, "you like taste beer?"

"Daddy!" Mama come all mad, not real mad, just mad voice. "No give da boy beer, wassamattah you!"

"Mama, I can make 'em like one real present? No stay Christmas or berfday, but can make 'em like one real present please?" Mama look at me and tell, "Okay, go get da wrapping and ribbon box . . . No, wait boy, come here first." And she tell me I good boy and how she proud I tink of Bobo. She hug me and I tell her, "Nah," but I feel good. Den I go get da box wit' all da old Christmas and birthday wrappings. My muddah save 'em from everytime get presents and da ribbon too. She lemme pick da paypah. Never have black and gold kine but had one with tigers so I went pick dat one even though was pink. Mama put da hat in one box and wrap 'em wit' da paper and I went help put my finger when came time fo' tie da knot.

Bobo was so happy when he went open da box. Was little bit big but he put 'em on and went by one car and tell, "Pape?" and da guy tell, "No tanks," and Bobo stay by da car and use da mirror on da side fo' make da hat good on his head, you know, so get one beer can label straight in da front.

"Tanks, eh. Tell you mama tanks eh. You sure fo' me? Tanks eh." Ass all he say over and over. And everytime when get green light, he take 'em off and look at 'em . . . make sure no mo' dirt on top. Me, I feel so good I miss couple customers at da red light.

So had me working da sidewalk and Bobo walking between da cars (my fahdah no let me go between da cars), and one shaka van went come: fat tires, mag wheels, teen-ted glass. Was just some mokes playing da tape deck loud and smoking pakalolo. I know 'cause more skinny da pakalolo cigarette and dey share 'em. One time I saw Cummings brother guys smoke dat.

Da mokes tell, "Eh, look da guy. He nuts yeah? Eh, go call 'em. Eh paperboy. Eh paperboy, where you get so nice hat? I like borrow. Ay, fit me good yeah? Ho man, perfeck dis. Eh try look, he stay bolo-head. Whoo, whoo, Kojak, man!"

Bobo he only stay try grab back da hat but da mokes only pass 'em around inside da van. Bobo try say, "C'mon, no fuss around," only ting he coming excited and no can understand what he saying.

"What you said lo-lo? You give us your hat? Okay, chee tanks eh?"

Bobo stay crying already and stay hitting da van, da side part. Pang! Pang! His hand stay slapping da outside and inside only get da guys laughing. I tell, "Bobo, nevamind dat, dose guys no class. Bobo, come already!" I like go get him but my feet stay stuck by da curb. I no can go inside da street 'cause my fahdah said no go but I like help Bobo.

"Eh, paperboy, paperboy. Here, I like one paper," da driver went call, and Bobo went stop hitting da van and go give 'em one newspaypah.

"No give 'em, Bobo," I went tell him. But he went give 'em and den hold out his hand fo' da money and da driver guy only laugh and drop his cigarette butt inside Bobo's hand.

"Fucka, you fucka," Bobo go swear at him.

Da light went change and Bobo he stay standing in da street yelling, "Fucka," until da cars behind start tooting their horn and da van driver only laugh and spit and den burn rubber away.

Oh yeah, da guy on da other side went throw Bobo's hat out da window. Bobo almost went run into da street without looking fo' grab 'em but I went hold him back and den one car went run 'em over and Bobo he turn and look at me jes' like was on purpose dat I went hold him back for see his hat smash. Bobo tell me fucka, too. I get piss off and I call him dat back but little while more I come sorry I call him dat 'cause Bobo no can understand dat good.

Bobo no tell me nothing after dat. He go by da wall and scrunch up real small into one ball, you know, and only cry. He cry so hard he begin to hit his head on da wall . . . his head bang da wall, but no sore fo' him. But I get mad 'cause jes' like my fault but not my fault, you know, and I know dat but I get mad at him anyway.

"Shaddup already," I tell him, but he no hear nutting. "Shaddup, I tell you! You no mo' ear? You lo-lo? Wassamattah wit' you? Mo' bettah send you Linekona School, da school fo' da mental guys!" And more he cry and more I get mad.

Good ting had one car went stop, green light and all, and toot his horn fo' one paypah. I tell, "Go Bobo, you go . . . ass Mistah Kim . . . he give big tip everytime." But Bobo still cry, so I go.

"Wassamattah wit' Bobo," he ask me. I tell some mokes went swipe his hat and tease him den dey went throw 'em away and da car run over 'em and den he cry and hit his head. He no can stop.

"Why no pick 'em up from da street?" Mistah Kim go tell me. "Ass da one in front da car?" I never tink of dat so I go get 'em. Look kinda had-it but still can wear.

"Eh, what about my paper?" Mistah Kim tell me.

"Oh, sorry eh."

"Here, you share dis wit' Bobo, go buy someting nice." And he gimme one dollah tip.

I went by Bobo and try give him da dollah but he only push my hand away and cry and hit his head mo' hard. So I went put da one dollah undaneath da rock dat stay holding down his paypahs. I went put da hat by his paypahs too. I went go back by da street and little while more, Bobo go real quick by his paypahs and grab da hat and put da one dollah inside his pocket and den go back by da wall. He nevah hit his head no more but he still went cry little bit. I knew bumbye would be pau.

So me and Bobo stay fren's again. He still wear his hat, smash and all and sometimes I go sell in da street wit' him (I no listen to my fahdah *all* da time). Good fun. We only laugh when da cars come close. Sometimes when he tink I not looking, he take da hat off and try fo' make da smash part mo' smooth. You know, he try bend da iron part back so no mo' wrinkles on top. Sometimes I tink though, what going happen to Bobo. He been selling paypahs long time . . . before me and still going sell bumbye even after I quit (when I get my skateboard and my college edja-kay-shen). I hope Bobo be all right. He gotta have somebody take care him. Maybe mama make him one 'nudda beer can hat . . . I go ask her.

II

One time after dat, one small kid went come by us when we was selling paypahs. He went put one box down by our newspaper pile, right next, and den he went pull out sweetbreads. Da stupid kid try carry four sweetbreads all one time. One under one arm, one under da uddah arm, and one inside each hand. Da stuffs stay slipping down so he go smash 'em wit' his elbows. Cheez, I wouldn't buy da smash-up kine bread, man, besides must get all his B.O. on top. He go come by us and tell, "You like buy sweetbread?"

Bobo's eyes came big. He like sweetbread, you know. He jes' look. I stay tinking he better wipe his mouth, look like he stay drooling over da sweetbreads. Mo' worse, da small kid tink Bobo like buy.

I ask da kid, "What you selling fo'?"

"Fo' school, fo' raise money fo' go feel' trips and fo' see feel-ums."

"Fo' what?"

"Fo' go feel' treeps, you know, escursions. And fo' see feel-ums, movies."

I went tell him, "I gotta sell carnaval scripts fo' my school too. You like buy?" I nevah sell nutting yet. Everybody in my class went sell ten dollahs worth at least. Even da smash-face, Shirley, went sell almost two hundred dollahs worth. She tink she hot. I tink her fahdah went sell 'em for her. But I nevah sell nutting so far. So I went tell da kid, "I buy one sweetbread if you buy my carnaval scripts."

"I like see your scripts," da kid went tell me.

I went show him my pack.

"How much all dis?"

"Ten dollahs."

"You crazy," da kid tell me, "sweetbread only dollah half!"

Bobo came for look at the scripts too. He tell, "I know what dat. Dat carnaval scripts, yeah? Good yeah, carnaval. Get anykine, yeah? Good, yeah?"

"Yeah. We go carnaval, Bobo. You go ask your fahdah fo' let you have some money fo' buy scripts from me and I go ask my fahdah too. Den Saturday after pau newspaper, we go see if my fahdah take us." I went make 'em sound real good so da small kid would like go too and buy scripts from me. Me and Bobo was jes' having good fun talking about carnaval stuff. Da kid was jes' looking at us, his head going back and forth, wishing he could go wit' us. Make him jealous, boy. But he only went by the cars fo' try sell his smash sweetbreads. I no tink anybody went buy.

Bobo, he only stay talk about going carnaval. He really thought he was going go already. I was jes' trying fo' get da small kid fo' buy some script but I no mind going carnaval too. So I was real nice to my fahdah and tole him I would help him wash and polish da car if he buy da scripts from me and take me carnaval. I tole him dat Bobo was going ask his fahdah if he can go carnaval too. Daddy just rough up my hair and tell, "Shoot. Wash and polish eh?"

Saturday, we went pick up Bobo, he was waiting outside his house. He said he no like go carnaval, dat he raddah go sell newspaypah at da baseball game. "My fahdah gimme da busfare. See, twenty five cents fo' go, twenty five fo' come back." Bobo said dat and den he just stand by da car scraping da dirt with his rubber shoes. My fahdah look at Bobo den at da apartment building where his house stay. He look long time den he breathe long and sad and tell, "C'mon Bobo. You come carnaval wit' us. You help Junior wash and polish my car bumbye and I treat you to carnaval."

Bobo came all happy. He smile up. When Bobo smile he make everybody like smile 'cause he stay so happy.

Had anykine, man, at da carnaval: plenny people, plenny rides, plenny food booths. My fahdah took us cruising all around da carnaval first. He tole us which ones we could ride (some was too dangerous he said, so no can). And he tole us which games was gyp (too hard fo' win, he said). And den he said he wait for us at da Beer Garden. No stay one real garden, just get folding chairs and one man stay selling beer. He said dat me and Bobo go half half da scripts.

Me and Bobo went cruise da carnaval again fo' decide what ones we was going play and fo' see which ones had da good prizes. Bobo everytime wanted to go back watch da guys chrowing baseball, but dat was da one my fahdah said was too hard fo' win. Had some guys chrowing, trying for win one big doll. Dey was making big noise and never let anybody else play 'cause everytime dey lose, dey pay again for play somemore. Da guys could chrow real hard but fo' win you gotta knock down six heavy iron stuffs, dey call 'em milkbottles. Dey jes' like bowling pins dat stay stack on top each other. Get three on da bottom, den two on top and den one on top. Dey must be real heavy 'cause even if you crack 'em square, dey no all fall down sometimes. Da guy dat was chrowing was getting little bit piss off 'cause he couldn't get 'em all. After he chrow his three balls, he tell, "Sucka, gimme tree more. I get 'em dis time." I stay getting tired watch da guy but Bobo no like go yet. So I had to stay and watch da guy somemore wit' him. Anykine stuff I went watch . . . how he hold da ball, how he aim, how he chrow da ball. He had one tattoo on da back of his uddah hand. I seen dat before someplace, three daggers tattoo. Pretty soon I went remember dat dat was da mokes dat went steal Bobo's hat. I went pull Bobo and tell, "We go Bobo, dry ovah here already. We go eat something."

"Play dis. Play dis," Bobo tell me.

"Nah, Bobo. Junk dis, we go."

One nudda guy was trying fo' chrow now but da guy wit' da tattoo was razzing him up. "You plug, you chrow like one panty. You call dat good? C'mon. You no can chrow bettah den me. Give up. Me next, me next." And he went try give da worker somemore scripts for play again, but Bobo went already give da worker scripts for play next so da worker told da moke dat he had to wait until Bobo was pau.

Bobo no can chrow hard. I know 'cause sometimes we play chrow-chrow with tennis ball but he jes' like me, not so hot. Only can chrow soft. So Bobo went try chrow but he only could knock down one bottle with his three balls. After Bobo went chrow da three balls, da moke guy went try pay again but da worker told him, "Dis guy went pay fo' three dollahs worth." I never know dat and I went tell, "Bobo, why you waste your money. We go already." But Bobo hard head. He only like stay and chrow da balls. Da moke guy get more piss off 'cause Bobo take his time and he only chrow soft.

"Yeah, why you waste your money. Pau already," he told Bobo. I no tink da moke went recognize Bobo. Could tell he was getting piss off though 'cause he had to wait and watch Bobo chrow.

Me, I went give up. I no can change Bobo's mind so I jes' watch him chrow. Jes' like he no aim. He jes' chrow as hard as he can, but still yet soft. Da most he ever hit down was tree, I think. And he take long time watch da worker guy stack up da bottles. I thought he was jes' slow but little while more, I catch on. Bobo sly, da bugga. He stay watching for when da worker line up da bottom row of bottles little bit crooked so dat get more space between da bottles on one side. Den he aim for da space 'cause da bottles fall down more easy on dat side. Bobo he pretty smart. Couple times when Bobo went crack da right space, everything except one went fall down. But Bobo went miss with da other two balls and couldn't hit da last one down. I was figuring dat my fahdah was right, dis game was gyp . . . no can win.

Bobo had his last chance for chrow and he went crack da space right-on again. Only had one bottle left and he had two more chances. He was sweating real plenny and he nevah care about nothing but da last bottle. He went warm up real plenny and make plenny form and chrow real hard but da bugga went crooked and never even come close. He only had one left and da moke went tell him, "You like me chrow 'em for you. I can crack 'em you know." Bobo jes' went look at da moke and I thought he almost was going give 'em his last ball. Almost I went tell, "Bobo no give 'em, das da guy!" But funny, I never say nutting. Bobo finally went say, "Nah," and wipe his mouth with da back of his hand and chrow real fast without warming up. I seen da ball hit da table right in front of the bottle and bounce off and knock da last bottle down. He went win. Bobo went win! "Bobo you went win!" I went yell. And Bobo was jes' smiling and clapping his hands.

Even before da worker went ask him, Bobo went point to the biggest stuffed tiger hanging from da string.

"I like dat one," Bobo went tell real slow and real clear. Was gold wit' black stripes and was almost as big as me. Was one happy tigah, had big smile.

Bobo went hug da tiger and went show 'em off to me and he let me hold 'em little while. Bobo wanted to show my fahdah right away so we went to da beer garden place and my fahdah went listen to me tell da story about how Bobo went win da tiger. Bobo never even like leave da tiger wit' my fahdah for hold so he went carry 'em around wit' him, even on da rides. And everybody went look at him. I bet dey was wondering how he went win 'em.

Going home, Bobo was talking anykine. Real fast. I couldn't even understand da stuff he was talking about. Only when we came by his house, he went stop. My fahdah came quiet too and went ask him, "You like me talk to your fahdah and explain dat I took you carnaval?" Bobo only went shake his head. He went get out of da car and tell, "Tanks," to my fahdah and den he went push da tiger back inside da car window.

"Fo' you mama. I win 'em fo' you mama. You give to her?"

"You sure, Bobo?" I went tell him. But he jes' keep telling, "Fo' you mama."

My fahdah went start da car and I went say "tanks to Bobo. Bobo was waving to us from da sidewalk, smiling up. We was smiling up, too.

WOMEN

When searching for themes for the monthly tapings, one jumped out and spoke to the *Aloha Shorts* co-producers immediately: women's stories. Line up all the publications from Bamboo Ridge Press and you'll see why. In addition to the hundreds and hundreds of individual pieces in the regular issues, the four solo volumes by Juliet S. Kono, the two by Lee Cataluna; the single-author books by Marie Hara, Mavis Hara, Gail N. Harada, Lisa Linn Kanae, Brenda Kwon, Christy Passion, Michelle Cruz Skinner, and Lois-Ann Yamanaka; along with the two *renshi* poems *No Choice but to Follow* and *What We Must Remember* composed by a four-woman collective; and the special collections *Sister Stew: Fiction and Poetry by Women* and *Intersecting Circles: The Voices of Hapa Women in Poetry and Prose* all testify to just how prolific and accomplished Hawai'i's women writers have been, and continue to be.

As producers for radio, there was also another very pragmatic reason for selecting this theme: the pool of fine female actors here on O'ahu, too many to name, whose talents were deserving of the challenges our local writers presented.

We returned to the theme of "Women" three times, always airing the shows in March, for Women's History Month. Just as Pavarotti did for the Break Room Divas, these women's voices sing out to us, "Vincerò!" ("I will win!").

Lee Cataluna
writer and performer

I think it's essential for writers to hear their work. Not all writers feel that way, but when I teach writing workshops, I usually include an element of performance or reading out loud. There's so much a writer learns by getting their words out of their own head and out into the fresh air when the piece is being read back to them. You die with every purple phrase and soar with every bit of poetry and truth. I write for the work to be performed.

When I was in the seventh grade, I had to catch the school bus from Kīlauea on Kauaʻi's North Shore to Kapaʻa High School. The bus was very crowded—sometimes four to a seat and people in the aisles—crammed with little seventh graders all the way up to hulking twelfth graders. And it was rowdy. Even the bus driver was mouthy and uncensored. I developed my eavesdropping skills on those torturous bus rides, with much older kids all competing to be the roughest and most outrageous, and I suspect that these voices came from that time.

When I read these pieces a decade after I wrote them, I can see how I was trying to sound like my idol Lois-Ann Yamanaka. I love the way she finds such beauty and truth in unexpected places and characters.

And I have a very vivid memory of listening to two teenaged girls in Longs giving each other life advice in the cosmetic aisles.

Corinna Molina – Janessa's Friend

Lee Cataluna

from *Folks You Meet in Longs*, first aired March 30, 2010

Ay, Janessa, try look da purple nail polish, you
should get 'em.
Match with your hickey necklace.
No act like you can hide 'em with makeup. I can see the thing shining
through like purple panties underneath white shorts. Shoot, not too
obvious you wearing turtleneck to school for three days, kudeesh.

Here, get the purple nail polish with the sparkle stuff inside and then get
the spray-on body glitter for your neck for da night time look. Get the
plum passion lipstick so you can leave all kind marks on him and no even
gotta suck.
Rub 'em all on top his shirt so when his mother wash clothes she think her
son was bleeding.

Oh, you gotta check out this lotion.
Look the lotion, Janessa.
You should get the lotion.
You no like chap.
You chap? You chapping? You chap planny, no, you?
You such a chappa', Janessa.

Look the small cute little perfume get.
So cute, yeah?
You should get that, Janessa. You should get perfume.
You should get deodorant.
Get the all-over kind, you know. You should get the all-over kind.
All over, you know.
You should buy couple.
Buy the shelf.

You know, if you put planny eyeliner, going draw the attention to your face
so people not going be staring at the muffler burns all on your neck.
Get the black eyeliner.
Not brown-black.

No, that's just black. Get the black-black kind.

That's the kind.

Draw attention to your eyes, that's why. You no like people staring at your neck cuz look kinda buss.

Or just buy the thick-kind scar-kind pack-'em-on makeup.

Put like Bondo on top your neck.

Make everybody think you hiding one zipper for keep your head on like the Frankenstein lady.

I no think so this even your aisle, Janessa. Come, we go find your aisle.

The one close to the pharmacy.

The one with all your stuffs that you need.

Maybe get some hickey cream right next to all the other stuffs.

Maybe get cream you can rub on top your neck for take 'em off so you no gotta sleep your aunty's house one more night.

I promise, Janessa, look so obvious.

Ginger Gohier (right) as Corinna Molina and
Karen Kaulana as Janessa Peralta

Janessa Peralta – Corinna's Friend, Sometimes

Dear Jesus please help me not eat so goddamn much
because I can hardly fit in any of my new pants.

And Jesus please help me lose weight so that I don't look like such a
goddamn cow in prom pictures.

Jesus, please help me not fall asleep in math class because I'm flunking bad
and if I have to go summer school I will be so shame.

Jesus, please make my mom come home late so she don't catch me with
my face in a big bucket of chicken and call me a fat-a-boola and make me
shame.

Please let her come home late and tired so that she doesn't even look in
the fridge and doesn't even check in the garbage.

Please let me be pretty and slim and beautiful and never hungry or tired.

Please kick my ass so I exercise and not sit on the couch when I come
home.

Jesus, please help me get through the day without thinking about lumpia or
won ton or anything fried.

Please let me think about other things.

Just fix my mind from thinking about what to eat.

Please help me lose weight even if I do eat.

Please bless my grandmother and make her stop fighting with my mother.

Please bless my brothers and my cousins.

Please bless my dad if he's still alive.

Bless that guy I hooked up with at the carnival the other night, Brayden or Branson or something.

Please bless my mom and make her tired so she doesn't notice anything.

And please bless me, Jesus. Please help me to not eat so goddamn much and to not swear because I'm sorry when I do.

Please.

Amen.

Lisa Linn Kanae
writer and performer

Donalyn Dela Cruz (left) and Lisa Linn Kanae
after readings from Kanae's collection *Island
Linked by Ocean*

I remember when a friend asked if I had heard my story on the radio. "They added Pavarotti and everything," my friend said. "You *need* to listen to it." That night, I rushed to finish grading essays and then found the clip online. At around two in the morning, I put on my earplugs and sat in my dark living room, listening to the incomparable Stephanie Keiko Kong bring to life the character, Cherie, as she describes her experience at a Pavarotti concert. Hearing Pavarotti's voice transformed my experience. I wasn't just listening to my short story. I was fully engaged with the story—cheering on Cherie, her friends, and the maestro.

When I hear my stories on *Aloha Shorts*, it's often as if I am hearing them for the first time, but when Aito Simpson Steele read "Swift Blur of Passing Vehicles," it was like listening to the familiar. Aito gave life to the father and son in the story for whom I have a special affection, and although I heard those characters speak over and over again in my mind while I wrote the story, Aito's performance brought them "home" for me. And for that, I am grateful.

Luciano and Da Break Room Divas

Lisa Linn Kanae
from *Islands Linked by Ocean*, first aired April 20, 2010

The loose change inside Hattie's pencil tray stay sorted according to value, and God help you if you no put stuff back where you found um. Das da kine secretary Hattie. Even her coffee mug get one designated spot—right-hand corner on top the first shelf in the cabinet right above the dish drainer. Nothing get past her—typos, subject-verb agreement errors—nothing. But about two weeks ago, while me, Tsuki and Hattie was ready for eat our Subway Sandwich low-fat-meal-deal lunch, Hattie wen snap.

We was sitting at the break room table: sandwiches unwrapped, potato chip bags torn open. Right before Hattie was going take one bite from her turkey on crack wheat, she wen freeze.

"How can you eat in this place!" Hattie shouted. She wen grab her napkin and started for dust the blue silk rose centerpiece dat was in front us on top da table and then she stopped and stared straight at me.

"Tsuki da one trying for turn dis place into one Ben Franklin craft store," I said.

"You're the one who said this break room was too *austere*," Tsuki said. "I bet you don't even know what *austere* means."

"Severely simple, lacks ornamentation," I said. "So whop your jaws."

Five seconds of silence wen pass, and then Hattie wen let out one low contagious giggle. Pretty soon, the three of us was laughing so hard, we had to wipe our eyes wit our napkins, but that's when I noticed that Hattie was crying for real kine.

"Can I get you something?" I placed my hand on her shoulder, but she pushed me away.

"Quit treating me like an old woman," Hattie said, and she sunk her face inside her hands. That's when Jayne walked in the break room carrying one salad and one bottle water.

Jayne is Mrs. Iwase's new admin assistant. The first time Mrs. Iwase brought Jayne by my desk for introduce her, I thought, cool, she look like my kid sista Elise—petite, little bit intense, but pretty smile—until Jayne opened her mouth.

"That's Jayne with a Y," she said, shaking my hand. "Everyone spells my name wrong, and I'm so sick of correcting people."

Tsuki, who sits across of me, was about to say hi, but Jayne wen frown at da collection of Happy Meal toys lined up on da edge of Tsuki's computer monitor.

Jayne proceeded to tell us dat she wen just pau her business B.A. at some college on da East Coast and decided to come home to, as she had put it, "help reverse the brain-drain syndrome on this island." In a matter of five minutes, we found out dat her fadda was one orthopedic surgeon, her olda sista was one corporate lawyer, her younger bradda was studying for be one civil engineer, and her madda was one retired Asian art professor who was one volunteer docent at da Honolulu Academy of Arts. I felt like I was suppose to genuflect in front her. After that day, Tsuki wen stuff her Happy Meal toys inside her desk drawer.

When Jayne walked into the break room, she neva say hi. She went straight for da sink and opened her salad container. Hattie wen turn her face towards the wall.

"Escarole is so bitter," Jayne mumbled, picking da curly-kine greens from her salad and throwing um in da sink. "I prefer radicchio myself," she said. "Subtle. Sweet. You know. More cordial." She had this way of flipping her hand like was one empty glove when she spoke.

"The last time I was in SoHo . . ." Jayne mumbled on about this deli by one canal, but I wen stop listening once I saw Hattie scoop up some scattered lettuce from her sandwich wrapper.

"Here," Hattie said, dumping da lettuce in da sink in front Jayne. "Have some shredded iceberg." Hattie wen bag from da break room.

"What's her problem?" Jayne shouted. "All I did was give her a budget to type. She can be such a control freak."

Tsuki followed Hattie, and then I followed Tsuki, who was heading straight for the women's restroom. I saw Hattie standing in front the mirror dabbing her eyes wit one tissue.

"I wasn't going to do this," Hattie said. She crumpled da tissue into one small ball inside her hand. "I wasn't going to fall apart. Not here. Not at work."

She looked in the mirror and found my eyes. I wen watch her face turn all red as the corners of her mouth wen turn down. She started for heave choke kine sobs.

"Clem and I," Hattie said trying for catch her breath. "We would have been married for forty years today."

One year ago, Hattie's husband Clem, who was an executive chef in Waikīkī, passed away from prostate cancer. When he was at Kuakini Hospital, Hattie only took three days sick leave: the day Clem was admitted, the day after he died, and the day of his funeral. She wen go even cut her funeral leave in half. Her kids wen fly home for help out, but she insisted on coming to work. Das Hattie. She one workaholic. She had to be. She wen pay for her kids go mainland college. Now Hattie's boy is one urban planner who live Oregon, and her girl is one multi-media artist in Seattle. They wanted her for move up Washington, but Hattie, she hardhead. She neva like impose on their lives, she said. For one year, she neva say one word about her husband or her grief. Me and Tsuki wen throw couple hints about counseling, but Hattie, she said she no like wen people meddle in her private affairs, so we backed off.

In the restroom, Hattie wen try for fix her lipstick, but every time she looked at her reflection, she would start tearing up again.

"What can we do for you?" Tsuki whispered.

I could tell Tsuki was ready for cry too; her nose was pink. Hattie pulled one nodda piece tissue from her blazer pocket and blew her nose.

"You need time," Tsuki said. "You need to be kind to yourself and heal."

Tsuki get dis airy, baby voice, da kine voice dat can tell da truth without causing damage. Her voice made my throat feel all tight; I started for tear up too.

"Take the day off," Tsuki said. "Take a week. Me and Cherie can cover for you."

Hattie wen rinse her face, took in a big breath and exhaled.

"Don't be silly," she said. She wen run her lipstick along her top lip. "You'll just screw up my system."

Hattie wen throw away her tissue, kissed us both on our cheeks, and went back to her desk. The three of us wen skip lunch dat day, and for da rest of da afternoon, nobody said one word about Clem, blue roses, or shredded iceberg. Even Jayne with a Y neva have anyting for say.

Da next morning, Hattie came work acting like nothing wen happen. Around ten o'clock, I went to da break room for grab one cup coffee, and I found Hattie's coffee mug inside da sink. And get dis—was half-way filled wit coffee. She neva even rinse um out. What wen really throw me off was I found Hattie's day planner inside da icebox. I was going return da day planner to Hattie's desk, but den I heard Jayne complaining about how da office's budget file was missing. Jayne had to go make one scene. She wen order Hattie for backtrack her steps, and dey found da file inside da #4 paper tray of da Xerox machine. About fifteen minutes later, Tsuki sat down by my desk. Total dread was all ova her face.

"Look at what I found under the sink," she whispered.

Tsuki held out Hattie's file cabinet keys and da payroll files. Her hand was trembling.

"Das it," I said. "We gotta do something. You heard dat frickin' Jayne bitching about da budget file? I was ready for take her outside."

"I would love to see her transferred to Security. One day with those braddas downstairs, and she would go crying back to college," Tsuki said. "But then again she has no idea what Hattie is going through. She's just . . ."

"One frickin' princess," I said.

"You were the one who said she was smart," Tsuki said.

"If my memory serves me right, I said she talk like one walking memorandum."

Granted, I knew Jayne was sharp. Could tell by da way she chose her words, but I would radda chew on one thesaurus den spend five minutes listening to her. She complain too much; Honolulu neva have enough culture, no more night life, da pace too slow. To top it off, she pushy. "Assertive," was da word Hattie wen use, but to me, Jayne wen act like she had one silver spoon so far up her ass, I could use her head for scoop sugar out of one bowl *and* stir my coffee.

Da one and last time I got caught in da break room by myself wit Jayne was da time she wen ask me what school I wen graduate from.

"Roosevelt," I said.

"I meant what college, silly," Jayne said.

"Well, I plan on going back to school," I lied. "Part-time of course, maybe next year."

"So Cherry," Jayne said, after she wen glimpse quick kine at my ID badge, "what are you anyway?"

"It's Cherie. Like da wine. Not da fruit. I Filipino, Chinese."

"That's funny. So am I," she said. "Actually, I meant your job title."

"I'm going to apply for a Secretary III as soon as get one opening," I said.

"Three?" Jayne said, eyeing up my Hawaiian bracelets. "You mean you're just a clerk typist?"

Just a clerk typist, I thought to myself. Who da hell she tink her?

"Oh gosh, look at da time," I said staring at my wristwatch. "I have a hair appointment. Buh-bye."

"I really miss my stylist in New York," she said. "I can't find a decent salon on this island. Who does your hair?"

"Fantastic Sam's," I said.

And you know what dat princess said? She said, "Fantastic Sam? Who's he?"

Me and Tsuki was on one mission: Support Hattie, bumbye she might lose her head or, more worse, her job. Our plan: follow Hattie around da office sneaky kine, so dat Hattie wouldn't notice dat we was watching out for her. When Hattie wen put her keys down by da Xerox machine, I wen tell her, "Nice your key chain." When Hattie wen place her memo pad next to da water cooler, Tsuki told her, "Can I see your notes from our morning staff meeting?" But dat Hattie, she not one idiot. She finally came by my desk.

"I'm going to the bathroom now," Hattie said, putting her hands on her hips. "Would you like to remind me to wipe my butt?"

"We was only looking out for you," I said, lowering my head for stare at my knees.

She pinched my chin for lift my face so she could look me in da eye.

"Knock it off," she said. "I'll be fine."

She walked away, but I neva stop worrying. If Hattie screwed up da payroll, dat might justify one transfer out of our department giving Jayne-wit-a-Y da muscle for throw any kine shit in my in-tray. What I needed was someting short of divine intervention. Das wen Tsuki came by my desk waving around da entertainment section of da *Honolulu Star-Bulletin.*

"Look at this ad," Tsuki said, handing me da newspaper.

I read um and laughed. "Since when you like go Venus Nightclub?"

"Not that ad," Tsuki said. "This ad. Luciano Pavarotti in concert. Hattie loves this guy. Let's go."

When I saw da word *opera* I wen give da newspapah back to Tsuki. "I no belong at dat kine concert," I said. "Dey going take one look at me and laugh. What da hell somebody like you doing listening to opera. Das what dey going say."

"You're being silly," Tsuki said.

"Go ask Jayne," I said. "She probably know all about dis Lucy-wotevah guy."

"Well, Miss Cherie with an I, E," Tsuki said, "It just so happens that Jayne already has tickets, and her personal trainer will be her escort that evening. Believe me. I heard all about it."

"For real? Jayne going?" I said. "More I no like go."

"Think about it. This will be the biggest cultural event that ever hit Honolulu and Jayne will waltz in this office yapping about how she was there and you were not," Tsuki said wit da most sinister grin.

Dat frickin' Tsuki.

I wen picture da scene in my mind. When Jayne asks me if I actually attended one classical music concert, I could tell her, "Of course, who neva?"

"Let me talk to Cecil first," I said.

Cecil kept saying "Poor-ting, poor-ting," when I told him about da Hattie episode, so I told him dat my concert ticket was only going cost one hundred dollars.

"Babe," he said. "Das one truck payment!"

"Cecil," I said. "What I did before I got dis office job?"

"You was one counter girl at dat drive-in," he said. "And now your knees no hurt from standing up for eight hours. You told me a million times."

"Hattie was da one who wen help me get dis office job," I said. "She da one told me I could do it. I owe her."

"You right. You right," Cecil said. "But you really tink one night out wit da girls going make her feel better?"

"Babe, you do da math," I said. "Nothing equals nothing."

"You right. You right," he said. "Good you guys go."

Das wen I got excited. Da last big night out I had was about six months ago when Cecil took me to his carpenters' union Christmas bash at da Pagoda Hotel. Was wild. My husband tells everybody dat carpenters know how for party. "We no sked get hammered das why. Get it? Hammered?" No get me wrong, I love my husband to death, but I neva ask Cecil if he like come to da concert. If no more pāpio in one net or his boys wit one cooler, den he not interested. But get dis. On da big night of da concert, Cecil, da love of my life, wen buy me, Tsuki and Hattie each one red long-stem rose. We wen walk towards da entrance of da Neil Blaisdell Center carrying our roses like we was born for hang wit da beautiful people.

Tsuki wen wear one killa emerald Suzie Wong-kine dress wit da long slits up da sides, and she wen even darken da mole on her left cheek. She wen look like one Japanese Miss Chinatown with her hair all beauty queen up—wispy bangs sprayed stiff. She lucky. She skinny das why. Tsuki can wear one rice bag and still look frickin' high class. Me? I wen wear da usual black skirt and leopard print silk blouse—well, was polyester, but no can tell from far. Frickin' Cecil. He wen make like he neva like me leave da house. I wen wear his favorite high heels; da ones dat, as he puts it, neva fails to renew our nuptials.

Cecil would have been blown away. Had choke beautiful women climbing out of limos and sashaying down the halls. And it wasn't like dey wen go borrow their kid sista's prom hand-me-downs. Those wahine was wearing everyting from gold tulle wraps to bar-fly sequins. I talking high-end showroom kine stuff, like da clothes get in da windows at dat "other mall" on da fourth floor at Ala Moana Shopping Center—Armani, Ann Taylor, Fendi. One time Hattie wen tell me dat she thought Ala Moana wen become one "socially stratified retail oligarchy." I told her I wouldn't know. I shop Pearlridge.

She may not be da type for make all high maka-maka and mighty, but she sure know how for turn some heads. Hattie wore her favorite Princess Kai'ulani mu'umu'u, da one she saves for special occasions. Da mu'umu'u is one classic: black wit one lavender and white wisteria print and black velvet trim along da low, scoop neck and da three-quarter sleeves, and super fitted for show off her slender waistline. Wen look pretty fine wit her five-strand Ni'ihau shell necklace. She wen pin one band of gardenia and orchids around dat jet-black hair dat was slicked back into one bun low at her neck. Hattie neva need wear eye makeup, just fire engine red lipstick. She still got it going on. All da sophisticated kine looking men was checking her out as she entered da ticket stile. And da usher wen wink at her when he handed her one program.

We each bought one glass champagne and walked up one flight to find our seats in da loges. Hattie sat between me and Tsuki, and we wen sip on our champagne like we was princesses or, mo betta, divas. Da auditorium had one fairy-tale like energy, like da crowd had one collective Cinderella mentality waiting for da prince for come and bus out one glass slipper.

"Thank you so much," Hattie whispered to me and Tsuki.

Her cheeks were bright pink from da champagne.

"We care about you, Hattie," Tsuki said.

"Yeah you," I said. "We no like see you get all futless over Tsuki's craft fair leftovas."

Tsuki gave me stink eye.

"I own all of Pavarotti's CDs," Hattie said. "He makes me hot."

We laughed so loud, da lady sitting in front us wen turn around and gave us one snobby look. Good ting da orchestra wen start for warm up or else I woulda clocked dat broad to da moon. As I listened to da horns, violins and clarinets play scales all mishmash kine, Hattie wen point at one couple who was right below us in da arena-level seats.

"Is Jayne into professional wrestlers?" Hattie said.

Sure enough. Dea was five-foot-one Jayne holding on to one hamhock-of-a-arm dat was attached to one suntanned Goliath wearing one too tight tuxedo and Oakley sunglasses. He musta been more dan six-feet tall and way more dan three hundred pounds. Da bradda had one balding hairline and whateva blond hair he had left was lacquered back in one skinny rat's tail behind his neckless head. He looked like dat movie star Steven Seagal, only more cheesy.

"Jayne could do way betta den dat," I said.

"Check out that gown," Tsuki said.

Jayne was wearing one aquamarine satin, off-da-shoulder, floor-length gown dat ballooned out from her cinched-in waist.

"Who she tink her?" I said. "Princess Di?"

"Oh when will you learn, Cherie?" Hattie said. "It doesn't matter who she is trying to be when her date has at least four hundred dollars worth of ticket stub in his hand."

We watched Jayne discover dat Steven Seagal wen pay four hundred dollars for sit on top two metal folding chairs. Poor ting Jayne; she had to gather up da bottom half of her poofy gown into one large, airy ball. She couldn't see da chair behind her, so she wen pass da airy blue ball to Steven. He wen look kinda pissed off because he had to stand up for hold her dress so she could aim her ass in da chair. Afta Jayne wen settle in her seat, Steven handed da blue fabric ball back to Jayne, so he could jam his massive body into his metal folding chair.

"He look like Hulk Hogan force for sit on one preschool toilet," I said. "I still say she can do betta dan dat."

"Maybe she doesn't know that she can," Hattie said, real gentle kine.

"Give me a break," I said to Hattie. "She know. I know she know."

I wen take one long sip of my champagne and watched Jayne look around da arena, as if she was waiting for somebody notice her. Den she wen wave at dis handsome Japanese guy about two rows behind her, but da guy had dis nervous look on his face and then he wen lift his program up past his eyes. I wen look at Jayne, and she was clinging to Steven Seagal like the bradda was wearing one flypaper tuxedo.

Das wen da house lights wen turn down, and da audience wen go nuts. Da conductor of da Honolulu Symphony Orchestra walked on stage and opened da show wit da "William Tell Overture." I read da program, das how I know. I wen actually recognize da song from *The Bugs Bunny/Road Runner Hour*. In fact, I was surprised I wen recognize planny of da songs da symphony wen play. Dis was da first time I heard one symphony in person. Da sound was almost too powerful. Was like watching one jetliner in da sky pass over da buildings downtown. My whole body wen shudder when I heard da drums and da French horns.

Afta da symphony was pau, da house lights wen turn on again, and I thought, is that it? Dey pau already? No could be. Da place was sold out; every seat from da arena level to da top of da highest row was filled. From where I was sitting, da arena looked like one calabash filled with people talking story and opening and shutting paper programs. After about five minutes wen pass, da house lights went down again. I tot I was going go deaf from all da cheering, whistling and clapping. Hattie wen grab me and Tsuki's hands.

"Be prepared to wilt, my dears," she said.

One bright, blue spotlight hit da middle of da stage, and one blahlah of a man wit one black beard wearing one white shirt and black tuxedo wen walk into da light. Rows and rows of screaming fans was clapping so loud, I swear da floor beneath me was vibrating. Hattie wen let go my hand, and she wen clap so hard, couple orchids tumbled out of her hair. Luciano Pavarotti opened his arms out to da audience like one Jesus statue. He wen press his white handkerchief to his lips and blew kiss afta kiss in all directions until he completed da entire circle of da arena. I wen wonder why everybody was treating dis man like he was one god.

"Hattie," I yelled, trying for compete wit da applause. "Does he do anyting else odda dan sing songs?

"He sings arias, Cherie," Hattie yelled. "Listen, you'll see."

Pavarotti sang at least five arias. I neva heard of da operas dat these arias came from, but I wen recognize dem from different movies. Like dat song "Nessun Dorma." I neva know what da hell he was saying, but Pavarotti's voice could rise and den fall and den hold one note for so long, I was force for close my eyes. Was like I was drunk. Den had dis part when da trumpets wen echo his voice making his words seem even more passionate. He wen belt out "Vincerò! Vincerò! Vincerò-o-o-o" holding da "o" part wit so much force, I felt like I was dat close to being pushed off da Pali. Da orchestra wen echo da vincerò melody—violins and cellos rising and rising, horns and drums got louder and more intense until dey wen hit da climactic end. Da audience went ballistic. Was like one thunderstorm wen split open da auditorium.

Hattie wen nudge me and Tsuki wit her elbows.

"Just like great sex, huh?" Hattie yelled.

"No shit," Tsuki said. "I'm exhausted!"

We wen squeal and wave our roses high over our heads, and I wen wish Cecil was wit me. I wen feel guilty about assuming he neva have it in him for appreciate dis kine stuff. Made me realize dat I neva need be shame about not knowing all da titles, da composers' names or da symphony numbers. I couldn't avoid feeling dis music; das all dat mattered.

Da aria I rememba da most was "E Lucevan le Stelle." Da song wen start wit one carefree kine violin melody dat made me tink of picnics at Kapi'olani Park or watching Cecil laugh wit his auntie them. But den, da violins wen stop, and in flowed da sound of one lonely clarinet. My chest wen feel so heavy, like I was longing for someting. Da music wen turn dark. Da clarinet and Pavarotti's voice wen do dis echo kine dance, and den da violins wen come back, only couple notes higher than his voice. To me, Pavarotti was singing like he was going die. I wen panic.

"Hattie," I whispered shaking her arm. "Try tell me what he singing about."

"He's in prison," she said. "He's looking out a window at the stars and remembering the times he had with his lover."

Hattie wen blot her tears with one napkin. I wen hold her hand, but she neva look at me. She stared at da stage, as if she was staring out at nothing.

"You know," Hattie said. "Clem loved me so much—too much, much more than I was ever capable of loving him."

She neva look at me when she said dat. Was almost like she was speaking to herself.

"Hattie, das da champagne talking," I said.

"Love had nothing to do with it," she said. "Clem was safe. He made life so easy for me. There. I said it."

How could she say dat about Clem? I neva know if I should be piss off or filled wit pity. To tink dat all those years, she was walking around da office with dat secret inside her heart. I not stupid. I not naïve. I know everybody get secrets. I bet everybody in dat arena had some heavy shit dey was hurting from. Could tell. As Pavarotti continued to sing "E Lucevan le Stelle," I gazed out at da audience. Even if dey was all strangers, I felt da sorrow in their faces—beautiful sorrow—as they watched Pavarotti sing about da stars dat da prisoner saw from his jail cell. No wonder so many people love dis kine music. I couldn't hold back my tears anymore, and when Pavarotti wen finish dat aria, everybody in da concert hall stood up and shouted, "Bravo, bravo!" Everybody except me and Hattie.

I leaned in close to her. "You OK?" I whispered into her ear.

Hattie wen pat my hand. "I just made peace with my demons," she whispered back.

Tsuki, who had already jumped out of her seat for scream hana hou, wen notice dat me and Hattie was still yet sitting down.

"Get up," Tsuki yelled. "What's wrong?"

I waited for Hattie for say something, but she jumped to her feet, stuck her two fingers between her lips and started whistling and clapping and crying. I neva know what for make of dat moment. I mean one minute Hattie is all *True Confessions* and da next minute she stay whistling like she at one UH Wahine volleyball game. All I know is dat Hattie was small kine off her rocker. But who isn't? You gotta be little bit nuts for pay couple hundred dollars so one of your best friends at work can make peace with whatevahs. So I stood up too. Whistled like da tita I am and clapped till my hands hurt.

Pavarotti's encore was "'O Sole Mio." Everyone was standing up and swaying as he sang. When he got to da second verse, da house lights went up and thousands of voices sang da chorus. Every man and woman who was there, from da cheapest to da most expensive seat, was like one Luciano Pavarotti singing like their life depended on it. Me and Tsuki neva know da words, so we wen fake um by singing planny "la, la, la, la, la, la" to da melody.

I wen look below us at da arena level. Steven Seagal was sitting down wit his arms crossed ova his chest, but dat Jayne, she was on her feet singing and swaying to da music. She wen spin slowly wit her head tilted back, jes like one little girl, gazing at all da people above her. She stopped when she saw me. She seemed surprised. She wen give me one big smile and waved her program above her head. Dat suckin' Pavarotti—he get um. And dat music. Does strange things. Miraculous things. So I figured, what da hell. I smiled at Jayne and waved back at her wit my rose.

Stephanie Keiko Kong
performer

It was February 2010 in Hawai'i Public Radio's Atherton studio. I stood alone in front of a full house, reading Lisa Linn Kanae's "Luciano and Da Break Room Divas," and I cried.

The Break Room Divas were a group of coworkers that I imagined as business titas quite like myself. I, too, don't really "get" opera, but I absolutely do understand the importance of showing a friend a good time on her birthday. Kanae's birthday girl had a wicked crush on Pavarotti.

For the titas-at-the-concert scene, the *Aloha Shorts* magic-makers elegantly worked Pavarotti recordings into my reading performance. As Kanae's ladies heard his voice for the first time, I gave voice to their awed reactions.

The birthday girl said, "He makes me hot."

In rehearsal, I worked to understand that line, but there in performance, with the swell of music filling the air, I got it. I heard the music through her ears, and I, Stephanie the actor, cried as those ladies cried.

The audience was there with me. Glistening eyes blinked back at me from the front row, and I heard distinct sniffles from the dark back of the house. I wasn't crying alone.

HARD TIMES – KIDS AND PARENTS

Bamboo Ridge's local writers are clear-eyed chroniclers of all aspects of Hawai'i life, including those that challenge us personally. Growing up poor or troubled or somehow jeopardized is the common theme of the pieces in this section. The two young people of Lois-Ann Yamanaka's "Name Me Is" reach out in inarticulate love as they try to build something out of, and in, pain. In "The House of Luke," Tyler Miranda's young brothers are allies in an uneasy local Portuguese Catholic household in 'Ewa Beach. The third piece, "Swift Blur of Passing Vehicles," one of several Lisa Linn Kanae selections in this collection, features a father and son struggling to figure out how they will live after their wife and mother leaves. The theme for Yamanaka's poem was "language," Miranda's story was featured on a show about the economy, and Kanae's story was part of a program devoted to celebrating the publication of her short story collection *Islands Linked by Ocean*. Together now, these pieces resonate through their shared compassion and heartbreak.

The House of Luke

Tyler Miranda

from *Bamboo Ridge* Issue #84, first aired March 3, 2009

Tide gets everything out. I'm talking everything. From the mud stains on Mom's gardening clothes to Dad's stink, after work, B.O. white undershirts. It gets everything out. I don't know how my little brother gets them dirty, but even Luke's soiled socks come back to white.

Ever since we moved back to 'Ewa Beach, I've been in charge of washing clothes. After school, at least three times a week, I load up the dirty

Daryl Bonilla reads "The House of Luke"

clothes and head outside to the beat-up Whirlpool Grandma gave to us. Mom says that I'm getting older, so I should have more responsibilities. One time, we went three weeks without clean clothes. Mom and Dad had a mean fight 'cause of it. Something about Dad being too tired after a long day at work with all the extra hours he has to put in 'cause of the promotion he took, and something about Mom doing the best she can at being a housewife, how she's too busy trying to do everything for the house: cooking, cleaning, taking care of the kids, shopping, and the list went on and on. Soon after that, I learned the power of Tide.

"Don't forget to use Clorox for the whites, Landon," Mom yelled from the kitchen, where she talked on the phone with her only sister, Aunty Selma. Why? She has no clue that I haven't used Clorox once. That Tide always got the stains out. I yell okay back toward the kitchen.

We don't have a dryer yet, so I have to line dry clothes in the backyard. I hang each shirt, panty, and sock, wet and limp, with clothespins, like caught fish hovering across the yard. Dad says maybe in a couple of months we might be able to afford a reconditioned dryer from the used appliance store. But no matter, 'Ewa Beach is hot compared to 'Ālewa Heights, so clothes dry right away.

Sometimes, my brother watches me load clothes into the salt-rusted Whirlpool. Luke sits on the outside basin, dangling his feet. Bites the nail on his index finger and nibbles off a piece. Crunches it into bits. Luke always complains about 'Ewa Beach. Recently, it seems like that's all he does. How hot it is. How he hates 'Ewa Beach Elementary School. How Mrs. Shelley, his third grade teacher, always calls on him, making him look stupid in front of everyone. How he hates Pupu Street 'cause there were no kids his age to play with. He slides the nail bits to the tip of his tongue and spits toward the fence.

There's a commercial for Rinso that I like where this old man and lady are hanging around the house. The lady keeps bugging her husband to tell her how he got their clothes so clean. He looks at the camera from behind his newspaper with a grin, pretending like he doesn't care, and then says, "Ancient Chinese Secret." She harrumphs but ends up finding out that it's actually Rinso. They both laugh as she shakes her head.

While we ate dinner, I asked Mom if she knew how I got the clothes so clean. She looks at me, clueless. "I no can tell you," I say, "Ancient Portagee Secret." I busted out laughing so hard, I almost choke on the peas in my mouth. Dad and Luke both laugh too, but Mom doesn't. She shakes her head.

"How many times do I have to tell you? You're Portuguese, not Portagee. You sound so low-class when you speak like that."

Now Dad starts shaking his head too.

When Dad comes home, it's straight to his and Mom's bedroom to take off his work clothes. That's three more things to wash: aloha shirt, slacks, and a thin white undershirt. When he emerges, he looks more relaxed. He's wearing boro-boro shirt and shorts. Pukas and all. His usual stop, before he heads to either the green recliner in the living room or to his work room, is the kitchen for something to drink. Sometimes it's a tall glass of ice water or a can of Bud from the fridge. Sometimes it's a short glass of Jack Daniel's. He said it takes the edge off. It helps him to relax, to get back to normal. Mom doesn't look at him while she pours the brown liquid from the bottle. Dad takes the glass and heads to his work room to play with his radio-controlled car. Mom tells Aunty Selma later on the phone that Dad never even said thank you.

I collect the shirt, slacks, and undershirt scattered about their bedroom, and take them to the bathroom hamper. Glance out the bathroom door to make sure no one is coming, then inhale the musty smell of a long day. Feel it burn from my lungs down to my stomach. It smells like a combination of Brut, sweat, and VO5 hair oil. It smells like work. It smells like my father. Tired and needing brown liquid to relax.

I'm supposed to meet Luke at his classroom after school. Mom wants me to walk him home. She says it's safer if we walk together. It takes me a couple of minutes to walk from the sixth graders' side of campus, so Luke knows to stay put until I come. But when I get there, Luke isn't in the classroom. Mrs. Shelley says real sassy and without looking at me that I should go check the office. Then she ignores me.

When I get to the office, Luke is waiting outside the office on the concrete. He's dirty. I mean really dirty. It looks like he's been rolling around in the dirt mounds behind the third grade wing. His new school shirt and shorts, all full of pukas. For a moment, I wonder if Tide can get those stains out.

As I get closer, I noticed his lip is a little swollen. His head hangs, but when he looks up at me, I can tell exactly what the problem is. He gets up slowly, and keeps looking at the ground. We walk without saying anything. The afternoon gets a little hotter. Without warning, Luke blurts out, "I hate dis school. I hate dis place." He kicks gravel into a smoke cloud around our feet.

"You like me kick their asses?" I ask him. Know it's not just one guy. Plus, I'm big for my age, but Luke's small for his.

"No, 'cause den I going be one chicken. No can handle, gotta call my big brudda. No worry." My non-athletic, Lego-building, artistic-drawing brother, trying to act macho.

"Mom and Dad gotta go office, meet with da principal?" I ask. He nods. "Dat's da third time since da school year start. Dey going be pissed. Not to mention almost all da clothes Mom bought you from Sears all bust up already."

"I know." Head low.

"What dey bugging you fo' anyways?"

"'Cause I look haole. Ev'ry day, same ting: 'Haole Boy, gimme your lunch money,' or 'Haole Boy, no look at me li'dat. I going broke your ass,' or 'You tink you so smart, ah, Haole Boy, wit' da nice clothes? Answer all da time. Like make us look stupid, ah? I going dirty you up good so tink twice and shut your mouth.'"

Don't know what to say or how to help. Search the ground for answers, but find none. Just the heat rising from the asphalt, sliding up my shirt.

"Today, I wen' get so fet-up wit' it, I get all nuts at Merril Puncion in class. Afta he make one sly *Haole Boy* comment at me, I tell him fo' shut up before I broke his ass. Full-on scream kine right in front Mrs. Shelley. Den Darren Furtado and all his boys whisper back and forth, 'cause Merril one of his boys too, eyeballing me dat whole time Mrs. Shelley writing me one note fo' da office. I seen Darren lip *afta school* at me. But dey wen' jump me recess time instead." A minute passes. "I hate dis place. I wanna go home."

"How many was?"

"Four. But no do nothin', kay?" He waits for me to say something. Keeps looking at me, but I have nothing for him. I feel him in me. I feel the pull of my brother's eyes, the pull of a brother I sometimes don't understand, screaming for help, but pushing further away, needing help, but wanting to tough it out. I want to help him, but he doesn't want it. I want to hug him, but he's so far away. All I know is I have to clean him up when we get home.

We round the corner of Hailipo Street onto Pupu Street, past houses with overgrown bougainvillea and gravel lots full of weeds. Silence. We walk up the driveway to our house. Mom was outside on her hands and knees, pruning one of her rose bushes. "Hi, Mom," we both chime in together. She responds without looking up. She's focused on the next snip. A rose falls on the grass next to her knee. Green streaks and brown spots all over her work pants. She doesn't see us go in the house.

Take Luke to the bathroom and clean his lip and cuts with peroxide. Tell him to jump in the shower. Pile his clothes by the back door and go collect the other dirty clothes around the house. Make a bigger pile. I'm going out the back door to load up the washing machine when I hear, "Landon?" Luke is sticking his head out of the shower curtain. "Why we gotta stay here fo'?" His question, so pure, so simple, so far away from 'Ewa Beach. I know he wants to go back to 'Alewa Heights, back to a familiar place with people he knows. Back to rainy nights and dew on the grass in the morning.

All I can do is shrug my shoulder and shake my head like I don't know why. His head sinks back behind the shower curtain. Back behind the sound of water pellets smacking a plastic sheet.

I've gotten good at hiding things. Since I've been doing the laundry, Mom never grills me about how I get my clothes dirty. She used to give full-on twenty questions: Where'd you go? Why'd you go there? What were you doing there? Who did you go with? You know you're not supposed to go anywhere after school, right? Just pick up Luke and come straight home. Haven't I told you there are all kinds of hoodlums roaming around 'Ewa Beach?

But since laundry has become my responsibility, I've started surfing behind my friend Toby's house. I've explored the sewer system down the road. It leads all the way out and dumps into the ocean. I've even burned some of the trash behind the garage. Mom never sees and never knows. Dad's paint thinner and lighter fluid are easy enough to find, plus the matchbooks he brings home from the hotels where his work conventions take place at are always lying around. Come to think of it, if Mom is on the phone when me and Luke get home from school, there's a good two hours before we have to be somewhere around looking like we're doing our homework. But make sure to do the chores before sneaking out. Chores come first, then homework, Mom says. A couple hours later, when Dad pulls up in the driveway, she gets off the phone quick. Starts dinner and makes like she's been slaving over it for hours when Dad walks in. Checks on me and Luke. She's always amazed at how much homework I have.

Ever notice how clean clothes right off the line smell?
Hot and alive like 'Ewa Beach. Mountain fresh like 'Alewa Heights.
Restored, but not really.
A hot so painful it's exhilarating.
Then back to normal.
Almost.

Luke helps me fold laundry. We sit on my bed, pulling tightly on shirts, making sure to get all the wrinkles out. Mom says it's embarrassing to walk around with wrinkles in your clothes. There must be a ton of shame people at school 'cause I'm one of the few without wrinkles in my T-shirts.

"You know what I miss, Landon?" Luke starts off, "I mean, beside my friends up on Skyline Drive back home?" He turns two socks inside out and squishes them into one, making a ball. I glance up at him. "I miss da rain. Da way it would hit da iron roof. Like a thousand birds running across da sky. Rememba when we would play out in da rain? I miss how cool it would get. It's too hot in 'Ewa Beach, yea?"

I nod.

I miss it too.

After first recess, my teacher Mrs. Kato sends me to pick up the projector from the library. At this time, the younger students are just starting to be served lunch. All the students are supposed to walk single file to the cafeteria, which is also across a field. Two classrooms of kids file out of the third grade wing and head toward the caf'. A couple second later my jaw drops when I see my brother dart out of his classroom, running full blast across the field toward the caf'. Behind, four other third graders, all bigger than Luke, chasing after him. Mrs. Shelley's yelling from the classroom that my brother is going to go to the office again for disobeying her. All at the same time, I want to shoot across the field. Tackle those punks. Help my brother. But don't 'cause I know he doesn't want it.

But I will if they jump him.

Luke reaches the lunch line, way ahead of the others. When he gets there, the boys all stop running and start walking. Watch, make sure they leave him alone. Right before Luke goes into the caf', I notice he's not wearing his shoes.

After school, I don't even bother stopping by Mrs. Shelley's room. I go straight to the office. Luke's sitting outside on the ground again. He gets up slowly where he sees me. At least he's not dirty. That's good. That means they didn't jump him.

We walk for a while. Usually, Luke says something by the time we get halfway down Pāpipi Road away from the school. But today, nothing. So, instead, I tell him, "I neva go Mrs. Shelly's room. I knew you was going be in the office." Nothing. Keeps walking. "I seen you running to lunch today." Head hangs a little lower. Still nothing. "I neva know you run dat fast." He looks up and searches my face to see what I mean. Seeing it, he smiles faintly, proud of the compliment. "Why dey chasing you?"

It takes him a couple of minutes, but he eventually blurts it out.

"Mrs. Shelley, dat's why. She so stupid, she dunno what go on in her own room. She no even know what *haole* mean. She tink da boys calling me somethin' nice. And when they call her 'da bestest haole teacha dey eva had,' she tink dey being nice. She so dumb. She no even know.

"She always collect our lunch money first ting in da morning, yeah? We all gotta put 'em in da plastic container. But when she give us our money back, and ev'rybody trying fo' get one betta place in line, she neva hear Darren or one of his boys tell me fo' give him my lunch money. Ev'ry day, da same ting. So ev'ry day, I run out da door before Mrs. Shelley say 'cause if I get into da caf' before Darren guys, dey no can do nothin' to me, bum-bye da cafeteria lady going buss dem. All Mrs. Shelley do is scream 'cause she tink we all playing around, trying fo race to da caf'. She so damn fat, no can do nothin' but make one scene from da classroom. So either I do dat, or I no eat.

"And you run betta without shoes, ah?" I ask, already knowing the answer.

He nods. Can tell he wants to cry. But holds it in.

"I hate dis place," he says, "I wish we could go home."

And now I know not only why his socks are so dirty, but how too.

It's so hot, that by the time we get home, both of us are sweating. We go straight to doing chores. Cleaning bathroom day. Grab the Clorox, Ajax, Scotch-Brite scrubbers, and Pine-Sol. Shiny porcelain and fumes that burn our noses.

When Mom goes to Foodland, I tell Luke to forget about his chores for a while 'cause I got a surprise for him. I tell him to stand in the middle of the yard and to close his eyes. The afternoon is still and hot, and dry, dry, dry.

I get the water hose and turn it on full blast. Put my finger over the hold so the water shoots out fast, and aim high into the air so that the water falls like rain over Luke. At first, he's surprised, but since it's so hot, I know it feels good. Steam starts coming from the concrete sidewalk in our yard. Luke spins around and around, swatting at the glistening crystal drops, trying to catch some in his mouth. He washes his hair with both hands. And for the first time today, he's smiling. I can tell he's not thinking about Mom and Dad at the principal's office coming up. Or about having to sprint just so he can eat lunch. I know he's not thinking about 'Ālewa Heights 'cause, at this moment, he's here. He's finally on Pupu Street.

Warm water pellets on a sweltering day falling from a beat-up, old, black water hose. Water pellets that pound the ground, kicking up more dirt and mud which cling to my brother.

Warm water and liquid sunshine.

I know it's not home, but it's the best I could do.

Name Me Is

Lois-Ann Yamanaka

from *Saturday Night at the Pahala Theatre*, first aired February 9, 2010

WillyJoe is a name
on a tree   next to mine.

He ask me to scratch it
in the curve of the branch

with the soda tab
he not using for the soda tab neck-

lace for next year's
Christmas tree, so I digging

and digging his name deep
into the tree until we scar

the branch all orange,
our names, bright orange scratch sap.

     If I was blind, I could still smell you, you know. 'Cause you always smell good to me. Like maybe Prell shampoo on your hair and Camay soap on your body and I know for sure you put Mums deodorant, the creme kine on your underarm.

     Or I could hear you, you know. Like right now if I close my eyes, I can hear you scratching and scratching on that tree branch all by yourself. Or I could hear you whistling our secret whistle, three times, from way down the street. The way I call you out your bedroom window at night.

     And if I was blind, I could still taste you down where you let me taste you, where I leave one big silva dolla size red mark. Yeah, I tink I know you good. So if God like know, I tink I could be blind. (And not mine too much.)

A name on my folder
in fat black marker

(but nobody can know)

so I write like Willy write
when he feeling proud of himself,
M L   LuvS   M E F

Mrs. Livingston loves Mr. Eddie's Father.
I hide it with my arm

when my Mama look at me;
I write on the school bathroom wall

and the next day, watch the janitor
paint us away.

Donalyn Dela Cruz and Kimo Bright are the
young lovers in " Name Me Is"

*Real lovers. Real lovers no sweat, you know. And afta, real lovers smoke one cigrette.
Real lovers, they shut their eyes, roll um back in the socket and throw their head back. Then their
mouth fall open. The girl, she wearing red lipstick. Gotta be red. But no tongues when they kiss.*

*Real lovers, the man, he carry the girl to the bed. She wearing pink with pink feathers
kine robe. He throw her down on the bed, you know. She bounce then sink like the thing real
soft. The music fade in soft first, then cree-shan-do until the screen get all cloudy. Then dee-
cree-shan-do.*

*I love you Mrs. Livingston. Then you say, I love you, Mr. Eddie's father. Nobody
going know, see? For real, nobody can know 'cause Mrs. Livingston, she in her true heart
love Mr. Eddie's father. And Mr. Eddie's father in his true heart love Mrs. Livingston. But
they neva let nobody know.*

*I could feel um. You couldn't feel um? The way they look and the way they turn their
heads for see each other? But you know what? Nobody wen' really know.*

Willy ask me write our names
in the black sand

and he run find a bamboo stick
so I can write cursive
the way he like
again and again:

> WillyJoe —n— Me
> M L —n— M E F
> LoVe LoVeS *LuvS*
>   *wj—n—L*

Over and over
until our names all smooth away.

*You know the shell bracelet I wen' make for you? I wen' pick each shell so could
be one surprise. I wen' choose only the lavender ones, and I saving all the browns and
pinks.*

*Then I wen' size um all in one row, small to big (like Uncle Penny tell me) til they all
even. And I sit on the porch with him last Saturday and string um slow 'cause Uncle Penny
tell I can learn the power is the Word.*

*'Cause each shell Uncle made um one word. For power. Like magic charm. I wen'
start with*

oral-ly. (send it by mouth)
Then petroglyph. (the name of one picture)
Infinity. (mean for-eva)

*I know the word I give for each shell on this whole bracelet 'cause I wen' name um all
for you. Each one. And the last one is you, Lucy. Lavender.*

My name on a matchbook
in his lumberjacket pocket,

he had um in his hand,
all night in the movie.

I have a matchbook too
with his name on it,

WillyJoeWillyJoeWillyJoe

but my math teacher grabs it
from me and reads it.

*Where you got this idiot's
jacket? I'm gonna call your mama tonight.*

He so mean. He says I love a idiot.
What's wrong with me? Wrong,

wrong with the love
I write on a matchbook.

Was pale thin blue. The Lucy on the palm of my hand 'cause I know you like I know the palm of my hand. Get it, Lucy? Was India ink with one reg-la needle and string. I wen' copy your name cursive like how you wen' write um for me on the matches.

I wish you could wake up in the morning and walk with me up the stream, way way up the mountain, the place I go by myself. And watch me cross the long wooden bridge and no sked for fall. I dive into the water, all clear like aquablue, you know, Lucy. Clear. You eva seen clear blue?

Gotta be na-ked or no can go with me to the stream 'cause I bafe there (without soap), my whole body smelling like one river, and when I look under the water with my eyes open, no so-wa, you know, and I going see you, clear as I see you now. I going see you. All. Feel so clean. Smell real good like one real man, you know.

Then afta, us can rest on the big boulders by the side and talk if us like live ova there for the rest of our life. Build us one tree house with three stories so that the wild pig cannot hurt us, Lucy. You can make banana pancake for breakfast, and I can catch prawn for dinna like one real family, you and me, Lucy, and all our baby up in the tree house.

I too stupid for you, WillyJoe tell me.
(But he not crying.)
Teach me to write.

Teach me so I can write
your name, he say, with the sparklers

on New Years the way I cursive
his name with sparkler

light all orangegreen
and smoke, a line of green,

it stay in the nightblack,
light for awhile.

Do it again. (He clapping for me.)
Again.

Me and WillyJoe celebrating
New Years by the school building,

burning our sparklers
and at 12 o'clock, he kiss

my ear. WillyJoe and me,
Happy New Year.

> *I stay singing to you, Lucy — in — the — sky-eye — with — diamonds. Kissing you there.*
>
> *The nightclouds stay evaporate, until the black so faraway. You eva seen one night unreal like Christmas time? Or maybe one night, like you was up Mauna Loa, and everyting seem so pull away from the ground so get more space between us and the sky.*
>
> *LucyLucyLucyLucyLucyLucyLucyLucy—Loo—saaaay. We stay in the sky tonight. My hand belong here. You let me leave um? I feel like you. 'Cause one day going have more than one hand. Promise.*

He take my shirt off that night, then his,
and lay face down across my lap.

I touch his shoulder blades, light
fingers first. Then broad and brownsmooth,
feeling good, good,   see

him shiver when I heat
the sparkler tip red
and ribbon it in the black night,

(He know what I want to do)

bring it down on his skin, burn
the first line.

It smell like herbs in the kitchen bottles,
the skin soft crackling like that and Willy,
he flinch at first,

then he thaw out heavy on my lap
so I heat the tip of the sparkler again
and burn his name on his back:

W
WIL-LY *(You wrote Willy)*
Sounding out the word

like I do in school.
JOE (*Now says WillyJoe*)

And he lick the crack
in my folded leg,
with every burn line I make,
licking up his tears from me,

and I smell his blood, taste um,
taste just like rust.

Now, he say, *Your name on your back*,
and I lie face down across his lap.

I hear the match strike and flame,
then I feel him burn me long,
and my body squeeze first,

then release the color gray,
that fall to my feet in slow motion,
gray waves out of my eyes,
in and out with the sweet smell
of skin burning.

No crying, now, Willy says,
but I taste the tears:
he writing best he can.

(As far as he know)
(As far as I teach him)

burning the main con-so-nans
of my name hard
into my back meat:

      L U   Sounding out the word.
      C (See.)   A deep, deep curve.

Sounding out the word
like I do in school
again and again.

I feeling all thaw out
in my bones, all melting
from what he done,

so he light a sparkler
and tell me write my name
in the black night,

and when the sparkler all done,
we both withering
in all the skin smell and blood,
lying on our stomachs

in the grass, WillyJoe and Me,
we no dare touch the scars
on our backs, too wet
to put our shoes on
'cause the skin might stick,

so sitting there,
swabbing each other's tears.

  Look what we done.

We walk over to the tree
and look at our names carve
for infinity.

  Look, he says.
  This proof for-eva and eva.

  I IS, he says.
  YOU IS too.

He turn around.

> *Look at my back, Lucy.*
> *I IS here too.*

I touch him.

> *WILLYJOE*, he says,
> *For-eva, right there.*

> I IS too,
> I say soft.
> I no like WillyJoe hear me.

I feel the thick, clear liquid
move slow out of my name
on my back, touch it

with my own fingers, feel
my name on my back

all the way inside.

> I IS.
> Ain't *nobody*
> tell me
> otherwise.

Aito Simpson Steele
performer

An actor is only as good as his or her material.

No matter what kind of skill and training, mastery of craft or advanced degrees in fine arts an actor might possess, he or she is married to the words that a writer committed to paper, and can only get them to shine if they are already jewels.

Similarly, writing is a lonely sport.

You craft words and sentences and paragraphs, chapters and stories, but the bulk of the process lives in your head—the voices you hear only variations of your own.

One of the awesome things about *Aloha Shorts* is getting to bring what skills I have as a performer to the fine writing from Bamboo Ridge books.

Now, there's nothing an actor can do to bring good writing to life or give it voice—the life and the voice are already there on the page. When writing is good, the actor just needs to speak the words aloud, and do his or her best to honor and respect the words and the truths that they hold. If not to give life and voice to the writing, then to give it body.

Perhaps the finest compliment I ever received as an actor was from Lisa Linn Kanae after I had read her beautiful piece "Swift Blur of Passing Vehicles." She said something to the effect of, "So, that's what it sounds like coming from a man." She was excited, and it was like she had heard her own writing from the other side—in a new and different voice. What had been so internal and personal suddenly had been given a new body.

It was good writing, and all the pieces worked to tell the truth that lay within it.

Swift Blur of Passing Vehicles

Lisa Linn Kanae

from *Islands Linked by Ocean*, first aired April 14, 2009

At first Shanoah thought the dog was dead. He found it lying on its side on a piece of cardboard, its head and shoulders hidden in the shadow of the Dumpster. But when he inched in closer, the dog sprung up on all fours and released an explosive round of rapid-fire barks. Shanoah jumped, but the dog abruptly snapped back since it was tethered to the chain-link fence behind the Dumpster. Shanoah recognized the breed—pit bull. And he knew he should've walked away, but he dropped his backpack, reversed the visor of his red baseball cap, and crouched low. He scanned the dog's surroundings. No water. No food. And then the pit bull lunged forward again. The rope went taut. The dog's bark punctured the highway's monotonous hum coming from the opposite side of the chain-link fence that quaked with every lunge the dog made. Shanoah bolted up the lane and headed straight for home.

He plowed through four clotheslines, dodging suspended sheets, shirts, bra cups, and socks; kicked shut an open oven door of an electric range left on the sidewalk near his mailbox; and then paused at the bottom of his porch and winced. The porch, littered with fallen money tree leaves, reminded him of an anticipated Ala Moana Bowls swell. If he wanted to surf that weekend, he knew he had better grab a broom before Pops came home.

"We not pigs," his father had often told him. "You gotta keep your shop clean, boy. Clean. This is our 900 square feet. Get our name on the deed. Yours and mine."

A year ago, after Shanoah's mother moved out of the house, Pops had become obsessed with neatness as if clean was a religion, Shanoah had thought. And although Pops rarely mentioned her name, Shanoah had suspected that his father wanted the house presentable in case his mother decided to come back. Pops also started lecturing about how their neighbors along the lane had to rent their apartments in the two-story hollow-tile buildings that seemed dwarfed in the shadow of a colossal wall of luxury condominiums so dense they blocked most of lower Makiki's share of the Ko'olau mountain views. "Nobody can afford a frickin' studio in Honolulu anymore, let alone one two-bedroom one-bath," Pops would say to Shanoah. "Our house is the last one left on this lane. You know how lucky we are?" Lucky, Shanoah had thought? The only thing that separated their house from the highway was a narrow, pot-holed, single-lane road and a rusted chain-link fence overrun with buffalo grass, ivy gourd, and haole koa. They were lucky, Shanoah had concluded, if some out-of-control freightliner truck *didn't* swerve off of H-1 at 70 mph, mow down the chain-link fence and come plowing through their living room. At least, that's what his mother would have said.

Shanoah hurdled four wooden porch steps to his screen door and then realized as he reached for his keys that he had forgotten his backpack near the Dumpster. He plodded back down the steps; direct sunlight heated his hair, shoulders, and back. That dog, he thought, must be broiling. Like a thrown stone skipping over water, he leapt across the cement block trail to the back of the house, snatched up an old hubcap and headed back up the lane towards the Dumpster.

Shanoah found a water spigot on the side of a nearby apartment building, filled the hubcap to the brim and walked closer to the Dumpster. He placed the hubcap on the ground, conscious of the rope's length, and then grabbed his backpack and crept a few steps in reverse. The dog lapped up the water until the empty hubcap teetered and flipped over. It wasn't full-grown, Shanoah thought, but it wasn't a puppy anymore, and it wasn't wrought with inflated pectorals or biceps or switchblade fangs like the pit bulls he'd seen printed on swap meet T-shirts and car decals on the back of four-wheeler trucks. But the dog had that classic boxy head, and its coat was light gray, almost silvery-blue, as were its close-set eyes. Under the dog's muzzle, a twister of white fur tapered to a point on the middle of its chest. It paced and yanked as far as the rope would allow, and then it lowered its rump and pissed.

So you're a girl, Shanoah thought. "I don't know who left you here," he said to the dog, "but I really should go."

The dog's tail swayed slow, almost leery. Shanoah took three steps closer, and the dog pinned back its ears. He gradually stretched out his open palm towards the dog's face, and it swabbed Shanoah's hand with several slimy, warm washcloth licks. Shanoah moaned as he wiped dog saliva onto his shorts. He lowered his left knee to the ground, and the dog burrowed its muzzle between Shanoah's arm and ribs until he lost his balance and landed on his ass. His baseball cap toppled to the ground, but Shanoah hadn't noticed how a gust of wind sent his cap tumbling away. His attention was drawn to the strips of raw flesh beneath the jute rope around the dog's neck. Shanoah tried to undo the knot near the chain-link fence, but the knot was tighter than he was patient, so he opened his backpack, pulled out his house key and started sawing, wondering what he was going to tell Pops.

In the back of the house, Shanoah unfurled a blue plastic tarp over a mound of soft weeds. He shredded a rag and used the strips to tie one end of the tarp to a water pipe and the opposite end to a clothesline pole, erecting a canopy that was about four feet off the ground. "Good enough, right, Girl?" he told the dog. "I figure if Pops lets me keep you, he going like name you Lotus or Viperette. Something fast and furious. 'Girl' is good enough for now."

Shanoah washed the dog's neck with Dial soap and replaced the jute noose with vinyl cord, which he secured to the clothesline pole. After he fed the dog leftovers from a teri-chicken plate lunch, he crawled beneath the tarp. Girl trotted in a tight circle, settled in close to Shanoah's leg and laid her muzzle on his thigh. She'd lift her gaze towards him every so often as Shanoah stroked her from the top of her head to the middle of her back. Her eyes finally drooped shut; her panting receded to a delicate snore. The highway noise subsided. Must be rush hour, Shanoah thought; silence meant stalled traffic on H-1. He heard Pops's pickup hit the potholes in the lane and pull up in front of the house. He listened for his father's footsteps on the wood porch.

"Look da leaves on dis porch," Pops hollered. "And how come I no smell rice cooking?"

"Shit!" Shanoah whispered to the dog. "I wen forget."

"You wen forget?" Pops yelled, "You like eat or what? And watch that mouth. I not deaf!"

Pops placed both hands on the base of his spine, arched his back and moaned. He spent at least fifty hours a week under cars, trucks and vans analyzing and repairing steering systems, stabilizer bars and shock absorbers. When his wife left him, he decided to apply the efficiency of a healthy engine to his home life since he had lost all pleasure in surprises. His routine: remove his shoes at the door and then peel away his socks on the way to the bathroom. Throw the socks in the hamper, turn the tap and dip two fingers into a pot of Gojo Crème stored on the toilet tank. He'd count to sixty, exactly one minute, as he kneaded the emollient in between his fingers, beneath his nails, his knuckles, up each elbow and then back down around each wrist—the perfect amount of time for the tap water to run hot. He'd rinse and then dry his hands with a gray-stained towel he kept on a pipe under the sink. Today, though, he inserted an additional step. He leaned in close to the bathroom mirror and with his fingers inspected the part down the middle of his head. The guys in the sales department were right, he thought. Tufts of his black hair had gone gray. "When the hell did that happen?" he asked the mirror.

Just a couple of weeks ago, on a Sunday after surfing, he and Shanoah had stopped at the supermarket. Two shivering surfer boys, shorts still damp, bare feet still breaded with sand, they waddled up to the checkout. After the petite cashier—cute brunette, Pops had thought—scanned the 12-pack of Coke and the tub of limu poke, she smiled at Pops and tucked a short brown curl behind her ear.

"That'll be $10.97," she said and picked at her bangs with her baby blue nails. "You and your brother have the same eyes," she said, smiling.

"Bradda?" Shanoah blurted. "Dis guy is my fadda!"

The cashier's smile turned into an O. Pops handed a soggy twenty-dollar bill to Shanoah and left the checkout stand. When Shanoah caught up with Pops in the parking lot, he cuffed Pops's shoulder.

"She was totally macking on you!" Shanoah said.

"*Macking?*" Pops said. "What is dat? *Macking?* Talk English."

"She was hitting on you."

"Shat up," Pops said. "She get one earring on top her eye. Wassup wit dat? What if da ting get stuck in my manly chest hairs? I no mo' time for dat kine stress."

"Brah, dat wouldn't stop me," Shanoah said.

"Tsah!" Pops said, humored by his son's bravado.

The memory of that pretty brunette goaded Pops. He looked at his reflection and tested a smile that lasted all of a few seconds and then slapped hot water on his face. In the bathroom light, his eyes softened from black to deep amber, like the color of poured oil. He unzipped his coveralls, stepping out of each leg, right then left, took a piss, and then put on a T-shirt and a loyal pair of faded Bermudas.

When Shanoah saw Pops step out of the bathroom, Shanoah positioned himself in front of the kitchen door with his arms crossed over his chest.

"Now what?" Pops said.

"Don't call the Humane Society."

Shanoah saw Pops try to calculate what was going on.

"They only going gas her," Shanoah said and disappeared out the back door; Pops followed him, looked at the blue tarp and then squatted low. He sprung back up, glanced around the yard and found an old tire jack and held it up like club.

"Boy, whose dog is that?" Pops said.

"Had choke blood all over her neck!" Shanoah made a clawing motion at his throat. "I wen wash her with Dial soap. Kills germs on contact, das what you said."

"Lysol kills germs on contact, not Dial," Pops said.

"Pops, I ain't spraying this dog with Lysol."

"I going ask you one more time, boy. Whose dog is dis?"

"Some jackass wen tie her up by the Dumpster. She was dying of thirst. Look her ribs. She stay starving. She was ready for keel ova. I swear. I swear to God."

"You know what kine dog dis?" Pops said. "You stupid or what? This dog is bred to kill."

"Not even. Check dis beauty out," Shanoah said as he smacked the dog's chest like a car salesman thumping the hood of a car. "Stocky, her body. Her legs still yet skinny, you know, like those 24 Hour Fitness scrubs. You remembah? You said get da kine guys who only bench press, but get chicken legs." He smiled; his father did not.

The dog nibbled at Pops's toes.

"She likes you," Shanoah said, swinging his arm around Girl's neck. They wrestled like two puppies until Shanoah fell on his back, his knees pointed to the sky, and Girl climbed onto his chest and licked his face.

"She's awesome!" Shanoah said. "She's da bomb! Shit, even Ma would love her."

Pops let the jack plummet to the ground. Shanoah sat up, ashamed of the mistake he had just made.

"Did she call?" Pops said.

Shanoah lowered his gaze. "I don't know."

"What you mean, you don't know," Pops said. "Either she called or she didn't."

"She neva," Shanoah said. "I'm sorry. I don't why I said that."

Pops retreated to the kitchen. Shanoah ripped away a fist full of weeds and flung them out in front of the tarp.

His parents started fighting when Shanoah's mother decided to take night classes at a community college. She was supposed to be earning an associate degree in business but seemed to be double majoring in bar menus and karaoke. At least, that's what Pops had said. Shanoah thought they fought over stupid things. Cigarette butts dumped in the trash can. Greasy fingerprints left on the icebox handle. Television too loud. His parents didn't know it, but he could predict the beginnings of a fight. First his mother would start chain smoking, and then Pops would organize random crap—coins on the table, newspapers in the living room, slippers and shoes on the front porch, his tools and collection of abandoned car parts in the garage. Sometimes Shanoah wished they would just yell at each other. He hated the silence.

Finally, one day when Shanoah came home from school, he saw Pops's truck parked across the street at least two hours earlier than usual. He found his father in his coveralls slouched on the sofa pointing the remote at the television set.

"What you doing home so early?" Shanoah said. "You sick or what?"

No response. Pops just stared at the television.

"What you doing on the couch?" Shanoah said. "Change your clothes. You know dat pisses Ma off."

"Your mother wen bag."

"So what else is new?"

"She not coming back," Pops said.

"What you mean, not coming back?" Shanoah said.

"Boy, you deaf? I said she wen leave us."

Pops pointed the remote at the television to increase the volume. Shanoah grabbed the telephone receiver and stared helpless at the number pad, realizing he had no idea who to call.

"Where she went?" he shouted.

Pops didn't respond. Shanoah slammed the receiver on its cradle and then bolted out the screen door. He ran across the lane, pushed his body against the chain-link fence, and, in desperation, searched the highway. When Shanoah could not pin down his mother's face in the swift blur of passing vehicles, he ran back up the porch and pushed his fist clear through the screen of the living room window.

"What the fuck?" he screamed. "You just let her go?"

Pops stood up, went to his room and slammed shut the door.

Two months of silence were followed by two months of rage. Pops and Shanoah had fought so often, the police showed up at the screen door on a regular basis. Finally, when family court threatened to place Shanoah in a foster home, Pops nailed the blue tarp over the ripped screen window. Gradually, like the aftermath of a storm, their home took on an eerie calm.

First Pops brought home a DVD player, which was followed by excursions to Blockbuster, where they were forced to negotiate over action thrillers or action dramas. Then Pops taught Shanoah how to sauté chopped steak with sliced onions and how to wash dishes with steamy hot water so the dishes would dry in the rack, and Shanoah taught Pops where to take off on a wave and how to rack up points on an arcade NASCAR game.

Shanoah was certain his father would initiate one of those man-to-man type speeches about misery and women that men seemed to share in television dramas. But nothing was said until the day Pops taught Shanoah how to drive a stick shift, something he swore he wouldn't do until the boy turned eighteen. The most important lesson that day was how to keep the truck from stalling on an incline. He directed Shanoah to the intersection at the top of Ward Avenue in upper Makiki.

The traffic light turned red. Shanoah pressed his chest against the steering wheel so his legs could reach all three pedals. "How come you wen pick one frickin' steep hill?" he yelled.

"You can do it," Pops said. "Just let out the clutch slow and then press the gas real easy. Balance um, boy. Hurry up before the light turn green."

Shanoah tried to coordinate his feet, but the truck bronco bucked, rolled back, and jerked to a halt. The light turned green.

"Screw this shit," Shanoah shouted. He pulled up the hand brake, lifted his feet off the pedals, and the engine died.

"Boy, press the clutch and start dis truck," Pops said, and he thrust his arm out the truck window and motioned for the cars to pass.

Shanoah stepped on the clutch and the brake and turned on the ignition. As soon as he released the hand brake, the truck started to roll back. Pops gripped his seat.

"Shanoah! Use your feet!" Pops yelled.

"My legs not connected to my brain!" Shanoah yelled.

"Shut up and pay attention," Pops said.

"I no like piss off da odda cars. I no can do dis!"

"Try shut up little while and listen to me," Pops said. "Just feel um give and take. Feel um give and take."

The traffic light turned red, and Shanoah surrendered. He let out the clutch, pressed the gas, and then, for ten seconds, he found himself in that exquisite place where clutch eases up; gas goes down; gears engage; truck lingers on an incline. The traffic light turned green, and the car behind Shanoah popped its horn, so he released the clutch and floored the gas pedal. The truck lurched and then peeled up and over the hill until Shanoah pulled over to the side of the street and jerked to a stop. He pressed his forehead on the steering wheel. He felt Pops cuff his shoulder.

"You had me shittin' bricks, boy," Pops said laughing. He sighed long and hard and then slumped back into his seat. Shanoah saw his father scan the view below— the Blaisdell Center's white rotunda, the metropolitan skyline of downtown Honolulu, cumulus clouds over the ocean.

"You know how many times I tried to teach your mother how to drive a stick?" Pops said. "I took her downtown, Ala Moana parking lot—you know, flat kine roads. Your mother could work full time, go night school, get straight A's, but she could not, would not drive manual transmission. I tried. I didn't yell at her, you know? I was patient." He looked at his left hand and rotated his wedding band. "I let her do what she had to. I guess she just gave up."

Shanoah wanted to say something about his mother, add his angry two cents, but he hadn't heard the usual bitterness or blame in his father's voice; instead he sensed for the first time the fragile timbre of failure. Even fathers, he had learned that afternoon, are vulnerable to heartbreak and regret. It was as if Shanoah had been sitting next to a friend, not so much his father. To make a comment about his mother, he had decided, would've been cruel. Shanoah pulled the keys from the ignition and placed them on the dashboard. "You drive," he said to his father. "You know what you doing."

It had been two months since Shanoah and Pops made it up and over that Ward Avenue incline, and now Shanoah sat under the blue tarp in his backyard feeling like an idiot for mentioning his mother's name. Why should he care if she would like the dog or not, he wondered? He used to steal Pops's beer and sit on the porch waiting for her to show up, to at least call, until he stumbled to his room too buzzed to care, and when he woke up, his head throbbed so much he hated his mother just as much as he had loved her.

"She not coming back," Shanoah said to Girl. "She lives three blocks up the street in one huge condo wit dat guy—pool and all—and she no can even call." He stood up and entered the kitchen. Pops, standing at the kitchen counter, had an open Budweiser in one hand and held out a twenty-dollar bill in the other.

"Go market," Pops said. "Buy her some food. And buy dry. No buy canned. Nitrates—no good."

"You serious or what?" Shanoah said.

"Take it easy, bully," Pops said. "I neva say we was going keep her. You cannot even sweep the porch. What makes you think you going pick up dis dog's shit every day? Go buy dat dog some food while I think it over is all I'm saying." He tossed the keys to the truck to Shanoah. "And buy her one collar," he said. "Dat cable around her neck look pathetic."

Shanoah bolted for the front door.

"And no forget for pick up one decent leash too," Pops yelled, but Shanoah was gone.

Pops sat at the kitchen table, and when he heard the truck bump up the lane he tipped his chair and rocked back and forth and back to Roberta, the wife who hadn't telephoned him or her son for almost six months. He occasionally saw her in Shanoah—the boy's eyes, laugh, frown, and hands. Shanoah had his mother's hands: sinewy and clean. She'd use those hands to lift her hair off of her neck with her arms raised, hands twirling a ponytail into a bun. He had enjoyed unraveling that bun, but he still felt nauseous when he thought about her hair fanned out over another man's sheets.

They were high school seniors when he and Roberta told her parents that she was three months pregnant. Roberta's father stood up and left the room. Didn't say a word.

"You haven't even graduated from high school yet," Roberta's mother said. "You have your whole life ahead of you. How do you plan on paying for this, Dwayne?"

He had paid, Pops thought, by watching his son walk around like a wounded animal week after week. Shanoah wasn't a boy anymore, Pops thought. The kid already needed his own deodorant and razor, and he even threw a few hints about wanting to go to college someday. "He one good boy," Pops said to the empty kitchen. "I get dat going for me. He one good boy." Pops tanked the rest of his beer and dented the can in half. He heard the dog's faint whimper outside, so he left the kitchen to check on her. He picked up the jack and then squatted to look under the tarp. Girl wagged her tail and panted.

"I bet you no more even shots," Pops said to the dog. The pit bull licked his knees, and Pops tossed the jack aside and massaged the dog's ears. "Give me one good reason why I should keep your ass around here?"

The dog squirmed and wrenched her head out of the cable loop. Pops tried to grab the flesh of her neck, but she yanked away and barreled over him. He toppled onto his back, and Girl was gone.

Pops ran out to the street barefoot. He looked to his right and saw the dog's tail disappear behind the electric range on the sidewalk. With gravel lodged between his toes, Pops broke into a hobbled sprint up the lane until he saw an elderly woman peering out her front door.

"You seen one dog?" he yelled at the woman. She pointed towards the Dumpster.

Pops spotted Girl gnawing at a flat piece of cardboard near the dumpster. He slowly approached the dog expecting her to break away, but she lay on her haunches and licked at her paws. He crouched down near her, and she plunged her muzzle in his hand, asking to be petted. He recognized the scent of Dial soap and then saw the band of raw flesh around her neck. Shanoah's red baseball cap, crushed against the chain-link fence, lay next to what was left of the jute rope. "That's just wrong," Pops said and fiercely fought with the knot until it fell away from the fence. He balled up the rope in his fist and shook it in front of Girl's face.

"You hard head, ya?" he said to the pit bull. "What you like come back here for? You no learn or what?" He opened his fist and the ball of jute breathed open and spiraled out of his hand. Girl grabbed the rope, gnawed at it and flopped it back and forth like a rag doll.

"Das how," Pops said, smiling. "Mangle dat damn ting. Knock yourself out."

He pulled off his wedding band and slid it deep in his pocket.

"If you hurt my boy, I'll—" but before he finished his threat, he slid the flat piece of cardboard beneath him, sat on it and held onto Girl as H-1 traffic droned behind him. He sat there, watching the lane for a familiar set of headlights. His son, he was certain, would come back that way soon.

ANIMALS

The full title for this taping was "Animals: Pets, Predators, and People" and there's a good representation of each of these breeds in the following excerpts. The performances are also prime examples of what the oral/aural medium can bring to the written word.

As you will see on the page, "Ma Ket Stenlei" could be thought of as concrete poetry, but it's also a piece that demands to be read aloud. At the *Aloha Shorts* taping, printed copies of the Pidgin poem were given to audience members, so that they could enjoy its simultaneous translation, as offered by Darryl Tsutsui. (Darryl admits to reading from his standard English transcription of the text, so that he could more readily bring sense to it.)

The performances of "Waiting for Henry" and "Kid" were some of our most memorable during the entire run of *Aloha Shorts*. Actors Jamie Simpson Steele and Karen Kaulana entered into the mind space of their narrators so thoroughly that for those who heard them, the characters became real people with real lives. Warning: real heartbreak ahead.

Darryl Tsutsui reads "Ma Ket Stenlei"

ma ket stenlei
bradajo

ma ket stenlei
dablucross wensen om
wong kreesmess kaad ah
hinostey nau bot
histey free eswy

nwen no damada bifo
eswenastey
veratenya shtrit ah
she neva lai kaam clos
shistey wyl
eswy

bambai shikaam pragnet
deng kaam stenlei
endabradas
dey stey wyl tu ah

mawnin tym
awach om pley
onda da chree
delai chey
da leev ah

wontym

damada

she weng get skwash

ontopda road

den stenlei endabrada

dey kaam ontopma step ah

stey hong gray

eswy

den slo... slo...
hilan... me... ta chom
bot not da brada
hisked

enso
me en stenlei
we wemek... fran ah
embambai
hika meen sai

we wempley fyt fyt ah
goo fon dakyn
aget shorech bol

awembai om
won smawlkyn supabawl
en wen he wac om
he bounts
enekympleys

wontym

amasmoor-ah

enstenlei

wadagondu weed heem

longlyma teeny krah

rambain feega

mobeda lan om go

ontopdamaunten

esmin hees free ah

nomodameng

gombada heem

so

apood om eensai da box
ena tydrom weeda shtreeng
ena jrup tudamaun ten

asin om waan tym
efta det

hilukluk wong ghos ah
hees hea

awl sten op

frana cold

hiloook me
bronz tym ah
jalyk
hilai talmis am lin
den
histergo

My Cat Stanley
Jozuf "bradajo" Hadley
from *Growing Up Local*, first aired April 24, 2012

My cat Stanley,
the Blue Cross (animal
hospital) went send um
one Christmas card, yuh?
He no stay now, but.
He stay free, that's why.
I went know
the mother before.
That's when I stay
Beretania Street, yuh?
She never like come close,
she stay wild,
that's why.

By and by,
she come pregnant.
Then come Stanley (from *On the
Waterfront*) and the brothers.
They stay wild too, yuh?

Morning time,
I watch um play
under the tree;
they like chase the leaves, yuh?

One time,
the mother,
she went get
squash
on top the road.
Then Stanley and the brother,
they come on top my step, yuh?
Stay hungry,
that's why.

Then, slow, slow,
he let me touch um.
But not the brother,
he scared.
And so,
me and Stanley,
we went make friend, yuh?
And by and by,
he come inside.

We went play
fight-fight, yuh?
Good fun, the kind.
I get scratch, but.
I went buy um
one small kind superball.
And when he whack um,
he bounce anykind place.

One time,
I must move, yuh?
And Stanley:
What I going do with him?
Long time I think, yuh?
By and by I figure,
more better let him go
on top the mountain.
That's mean he's free, yuh?
No more the mans
going bother him.

So,
I put um inside the box,
and I tied um with the string,
and I drove to the mountain.

I seen um one time
after that.
He look like one ghost, yuh?

His hair
all stand up
from the cold.

He look me
long time, yuh?
Just like
he like tell me something.

Then,
he stay go.

Waiting for Henry
Gail N. Harada
from *The Best of Bamboo Ridge*, first aired April 24, 2012

I like the feel of a cat's head, the fur close to the bone. I like the feel of a cat's skull, the shape of it. It is soothing to stroke a cat on the broad flat forehead, feeling the sculpted surfaces under the fur. The tips of a cat's ears are cool. My fingers run through the fur of cats.

I have one lover and one cat. I call my cat Henry after O. Henry and Henry James. My lover is named Jonathan Henry. After his grandfather. Sometimes I call him Henry because it is so much simpler than trying to say Jonathan. And sometimes I call him Jon.

Henry my cat rejects me all the time. Come to me, baby, come to me, lover, I say. He walks away, tail twitching high. I can see his lightly furred two-toned cat balls when he walks away. I think they are so precious. Cat balls are so cute. Henry knows I love him. That is why he can scratch me and make me bleed. That is why he rejects me so much. Cats are like that sometimes.

Jon my lover, the other Henry, is very patient all the time. Sometimes I wonder what he is thinking; he is always so terribly tactful. He is strong but not heavily muscled. Some would call him a "prize catch" (he is a promising medical student), but I would prefer not to look at him that way. Maybe I love Jonathan Henry. He never rejects me. Some people are like that.

During the afternoon, after work, I play with Henry my cat. I rub him and stroke his head. His beautiful head. I tickle his stomach and admire his cute cat balls. I carry him around the house checking the windows. I secure the latches of the screens in the kitchen and the bathroom. I do not want Henry to leave me. I do not want him to be hit by a car.

At night, Henry my lover comes. In the dark, we play out our passions. We become sticky with sweat and fall asleep with the covers off our bodies. Sometimes I feel that Henry my cat is watching us, and I feel embarrassed and somehow wanton. When I make love with Henry the man, I have to close my eyes to enjoy it. I am afraid that if I open them, I will see Henry my cat staring at us, his eyes glowing in the dark.

It is a morning like other mornings. As usual, Henry my lover is ignoring Henry my cat. Henry my lover sits on the couch reading the morning paper. Henry my cat is sitting in the other corner staring at Henry my lover. They are so ridiculous looking, that pair of Henrys. Especially Henry my cat. He looks positively furious, twitching his tail at Henry my lover like that.

Softly I say, teasing, "Henry."

Henry my lover looks at me and says, "Why do you talk to your dumb cat like that? It's abnormal and unhealthy. Stupid cat."

He is not usually so touchy.

Henry my lover has never stroked Henry my cat's beautiful sleek head. He does not like cats. They make him uncomfortable. Perhaps he sees Henry my cat staring with amber eyes at us when we make love at night.

Henry my lover is asking me a very important question, one he has asked me several times before, one which I have never yet answered.

"Crystal, will you marry me?"

"Maybe."

"When?"

"I don't know." I always answer like this. It makes it sound like I do not care. But I do.

"When will you know?"

Jonathan is getting angry. I can tell. He is trying to control his anger. Why doesn't he just swear at me or something? I do not know what to tell him. How should I know when I will be sure? I do not even know if I really love him. What does it mean, to love?

"I don't know when I will know."

A pause. Jonathan looks at me with a suffering face.

"Do you love me?" he asks.

"Yes," I lie. I cannot stand that hurt look in his eyes. I wish he would talk about something else.

"What more is there?"

"It's not that simple," I say.

"Why?"

I pause, feeling the panic in my stomach spread. Sometimes Jonathan makes me feel cornered. He is always demanding that I explain myself to him.

"I don't know you," I say. I feel miserable. I wonder what put these particular words into my mouth. I wish that Henry my cat was here so that I would have something to do with my hands and something to look at besides Henry my lover's face and my feet. I say things that I know will provoke Jonathan. I say things that will hurt him. Is it because these things are true? I say again, "I don't really know you."

He laughs a short bitter laugh. It is a hard, unpleasant sound. Softly he says, "You don't know me." He is incredulous. I am sorry I said that. Now it is his turn to hurt me.

"You say you love me when you don't even know me? You sleep with me without knowing me. Come now, surely you can marry me too without knowing me."

I cannot stand his sarcastic tone of voice.

"No!" I say. "No. You don't understand."

"I don't think I'll ever understand you, Crystal."

I start to cry. I want to scream at Jonathan. How does he know that he loves me? But I am afraid he will say that he really does not love me.

Jonathan holds me gently in his arms.

"I think I love you, Crystal. But if you don't love me, I'm just wasting my time . . ." his voice trails off. He sounds so sad and tired.

I wish things were nice and perfect. I wish I could say yes and make things simple. Sometimes I wish Jonathan would leave me alone. Sometimes I wish I never got to know him this way.

Henry my lover has left me. I do not like to think about the reasons why he left. I suppose I have driven him to it. Ever since he first started coming at night, in the dark, I have been slowly pushing him away. I was not really aware of what I was doing. Maybe I was just fooling myself into thinking that despite all the trying things about me, Jonathan would still wait for me to make up my mind. Now he is gone.

There was no big quarrel at the end. He was so damn tactful and nice about saying that things had gotten to the point where he did not enjoy being with me. I never meant to irritate him. He told me he thought we should get to know other people who might be more suited to us. He said it would be better for me. I did not cry until he walked out the door. His last words were so trite I would laugh if it did not hurt so much. "We can still be friends," he said before he left. Standard farewell lines. "I'll be seeing you," he said, as if nothing at all had ever happened. I never want to see him again.

Do I love him?

I talk with Henry my cat. I caress his head and tell him silly things. "Oh Henry Henry Henry. You'll never leave me, will you?" He miaows at me. I miaow back at him and laugh. I spend the night watching television with Henry on my lap. Nothing I watch makes much of an impression on me. I talk to Henry my cat while the television goes on. I predict the eventual outcomes of each situation comedy and each serial. I laugh at the commercials. I tell Henry my cat what a lady-killer he is. I tell him what a handsome handsome tiger he is. I get tired of the television. I take Henry my cat with me to my bedroom. I want to lie down. I find one of Jonathan's socks on the floor by my bed. I start crying. I miss his dark shape and his breathing by my pillow. Henry my cat just looks at me. He purrs and rubs his head against my hand. What would I do without him?

Instead of going to sleep, I play some more with Henry my cat. I cannot sleep. I run through the silent rooms, breaking the stillness with my running feet while Henry my cat chases me. Laughing, I run over the chairs and tables in the living room and the dining room. I leap on the kitchen counters. I laugh as I cavort all over the house with Henry my cat at my heels. It is three o'clock in the morning as the sound of my laughter fades. The house becomes very quiet. I pick up Henry my cat and cradle him like a baby. I think I miss Henry my lover. Suddenly I feel very lonely.

I think I hear noises in the parlor. I go cautiously with Henry my cat to check. It is only the curtain billowing with the breeze and scraping against the lampshade.

Three days later, I come home to an empty house after shopping. Henry my cat is gone. I do not know how he could have left. I am always very careful to secure all the windows before I go out. I open all the cupboards and all the closets. I call for Henry. I run around the house calling for Henry. I wail for Henry Henry. I run around the block calling for him. I walk back to my place, telling myself that Henry is all right and he will come back.

That night I wait for Henry my cat. I try not to think about cars and cat-nappers. I try not to think of how empty the house is. I do not want my Henry to be squashed to death beneath the wheels of some car. I do not want him to be dissected in some biology class. I do not want him to end up as part of some woman's fur coat. I have kept him so carefully. And now he is gone. He has left me and I am alone.

I hear cats crying nearby. Henry? I run outside and start calling again for Henry my cat. I see the cats but Henry my cat is not with them. I go back inside the house, listening for Henry. There is a faint rustling noise outside. Henry? "Henry!" But it is only the wind blowing the leaves in the trees.

Who would think the night could be filled with such sounds? I hear all the leaves that move with each passing night breeze. I can hear the crickets that are rubbing their wings together and vibrating their dry little bodies.

I fall asleep waiting for Henry. I have a dream. I dream of a black panther who comes near my bed, who comes with the night. His fur ripples over his big panther bones. He glistens in the dark. I am afraid of him. I touch his head. It is smooth. I lose my fear of him in his beautiful head. His fur is thick and seems to perpetually flow over his skull. His eyes are brown, like the eyes of Henry my lover. But this is not Henry my lover. This is a strong panther. He stands by my bed as I stroke his perfect head. His ears are rounded at their cool tips. The fur on his body is also cool. It makes me think of mountain springs and of dew on grass. He is so still. He stands patiently while I run my fingers through his rich black fur.

Henry my cat walks into the room. He is light and glistening. He is so small next to this panther. He is so tiny the panther could probably kill him by simply stepping on him. The panther and Henry my cat start stalking each other. I do not know whether this is a game or not. I watch them gliding in their circles. I watch their immobile cat faces as they slide their soft paws over the smooth vinyl floor. It seems that they will forever glide and slither in their circles on their padded feet. I remember that their velvet paws hide claws.

The panther raises one paw. He raises it like a club. I think he is going to club Henry my cat senseless; he will beat Henry my cat to death. I see the claws coming out of hiding. They gleam and flash. Cats are very clean. I see now that the panther is going to take the life out of Henry my cat with one clean and neat swipe of his claws. I want to save Henry my cat. I cannot move or scream. I am helpless as the panther's paw begins its descent towards Henry my cat. I cannot even close my eyes.

Suddenly, I see that it is the panther who is the victim after all. Henry my cat is under the panther. His tiny claws are moving upward in an arc. He is going to scratch the belly of the panther. I am afraid I will have to see the panther's guts spill out. I am afraid that the pink guts will fall on Henry my cat and suffocate him. The big panther will fall on Henry my cat and crush him. I do not want Henry my cat to die. I do not want the panther to die. I want to save them. Henry my cat's claws flash like little mirrors as they continue upward. The panther's claws look like curved jewels, gleaming with the light of a hundred suns and stars, as they continue downward. I want everything to stop now. I want everything to start over again and end differently. I want everything to stop. Stop. Stop.

When I wake, I hear myself saying Henry Henry Henry. I reach for Henry my lover but he is not here. I want his arms around me. I want him. Why did I lie to him? I told him that I did not love him. Maybe I did not lie to him after all. Maybe I really do not love him. I do not know. Henry Henry. Maybe I mean Henry my cat. I miss Henry my cat. Where did Henry my cat go? How did he go? Henry my cat, if you come back I will feed you good tuna every day. I will let you play outside more often. Henry. Henry my lover, if you come back I will even marry you. I will love you. I will be a good wife. And I will always call you Jonathan instead of Henry. Please come back.

The next morning, over a solitary cup of coffee, I consider an ad I could put in the classified section of the newspaper. "Lost: one cat and one lover. Call ————." People would only snicker. I would be plagued by obscene phone calls all hours of the day and night. Besides, neither Jonathan nor Henry my cat ever reads the classified ads. I rip the ad into little flakes of paper.

I wait for Henry.

Kid

Lois-Ann Yamanaka

from *Saturday Night at the Pahala Theatre*, first aired May 8, 2012

Bernie and Melvin went up Mauna Kea
couple weeks ago for hunt goat.
They was going make smoke meat
for Melvin's bradda's grad party.
Bernie say they was going over this small lava hill
when they wen' spark one big herd.
But end up Bernie wen' shoot one lady goat
and when he went up near her,
had one small baby goat
crying where the madda was dead.
Bernie say the baby no mo than few days old.

So he bring um back to the shop with him.
Bumbye the baby ma-ke die dead,
no mo mommy, no can eat grass yet.
Bernie give the baby to me.
He buy one whole case of the small
Carnation milks and one baby bottle.
Then he show me how make
half and a half Carnation milk with warm water.
Then how for test um if too hot on my arm.
Bernie say no can be Carnation powder milk
or else the goat get biri-biri.

Bernie put one old blanket on the floor
of the shop and the baby goat,
she sit on my lap when I feed her.
She attack the bottle and by the side of her mouth
get milk bubbles. She kick her legs when she eat
and she make funny kine sounds,
but I smell her neck and kiss her all over.
Goats get a real goat smell.
I smell the sheeps before in Bernie's shop
but they no smell like my goat.
I tell Bernie I call the baby, Lambie.

He say baby goats ain't called lambs.
They call um *kids*.
Baby sheeps is lambs.
I tell him I no care.
She is one lamb to me.

In the morning, I rush to the shop
so I can feed Lambie. When I go school,
I smell like one goat.
Lunch time, I use my home lunch pass
but I no go home.
I go the shop feed Lambie.
Bernie, he make me tuna sandwich or grill cheese
and I eat um on my way back to school.
After school, I run over there
and Lambie, she see me coming
and she wag her tail like one dog
and she prance sideways on all four hoofs.
She knock over Bernie's tools, his knifes,
and some newspapers. Bernie say pretty soon,
I have to take her home and tie her
in the backyard so she can eat grass.
Plus, he say, he tired of sweeping up
goat Raisinets from his floor.

So Bernie and me take Lambie to my house in the Jeep.
He get one big oil drum, hollow out,
for Lambie sleep inside.
Bernie say gotta move her around the yard
every week and he show me how.
My madda, she hate Lambie.
She think I nuts stay out there
with my goat till 8:00 at night.
She yelling from the window,
Get in this fricken house.
You think you one goat or what?
Then she tell me if she step on one goat shit
when she hanging laundry, I going get lickens
so I no put Lambie by the clothesline.

Now Bernie say he not going give me
no mo pets 'cause I ditch him.
He say I no visit his shop,
I no sweep for him no mo,
and no mo nobody for talk story with.
I go home and I feel bad
but I come happy when I see Lambie.
But what I seen that day,
I no could believe.
Lambie had eat all my madda's
wild violet hedges by the washing machine
and my madda wen' rake up
all the goat shit in one big pile
next to the hedges.

My madda no even come outside when she yell,
You and your old man friend, Bernie,
better do something about that fricken goat
or I going give um to the old men
across the street and they going eat um.
Stay fuckin' stinkin' up my whole yard.
Get rid of um. Now.

Bernie say we cannot take Lambie
back to the mountains 'cause she too tame.
She no can survive already.
He say his backyard too many of his hunting dogs
so Bernie, he call his friend
at the Onekahakaha Zoo in Hilo.
The man tell we can take Lambie live over there.

Long, the ride to Hilo.
Lambie, she know something wrong.
When we take her in the zoo,
all the peoples watch 'cause she follow me
like one dog on a leash.
The zoo man, he lead Lambie into the big goat cage.
Bernie say the goat cage look exactly
like the place he find Lambie

but I know he trying for make me feel better.
Then he treat me ice shave
from the truck but I no can take even one bite.
I hold um by my lips all cold
when I look at the cage.

The big billies, they surround Lambie.
She looking around for run away.
Then she see me. She cry one cry
I neva going forget in my whole life.
One big, long bleat.
She run over the lava rock hill
close to the side of the cage I stay by.
The billies all follow her.
They smell the human hands on her.
They smell her all over.
She back up against the fence.
Leave her alone, I tell.
Bernie, help her.
She, she just one kid.

REAL AND SURREAL

When looking for pieces to fit the themes for shows, we'd either remember or run across some downright . . . unusual writing that we just had to include. In this section, the pieces share some slightly unreal qualities. Humor is often an important element in these pieces, ranging from the funny and spooky Halloween some local kids experience in Darrell H.Y. Lum's "Toads," to Cedric Yamanaka's account of the life of Oz Kalani, a bit player on the original *Hawaii Five-O*. Things get jittery in "A Day in da Life of a Java Junkie," a piece by Lisa Linn Kanae about a woman's relationship to caffeine. And we visit the full-on surreal with Lanning C. Lee's tough cockroach survivor in "Too Smart to Slow Down," and in Denise Duhamel's "Apocalyptic Barbie," both producer favorites.

Apocalyptic Barbie
Denise Duhamel
from *Bamboo Ridge* Issue #60, first aired November 15, 2011

Barbie didn't need air like the others.
Some of her sisters melted during the explosion,
but this Barbie had been tossed in a damp rumpus room
under a pile of moldy books. *I thought those missiles
were destroyed*, she heard the human husband scream
just before he burst into flames. *What about the treaty?*
cried the wife and the little girl. This was sad,
thought Barbie who felt unusually detached.
Maybe she was in shock. Maybe her emotions
were nuclear-tampered. She wished she could run
away from it all, and for the first time, her wish came true.
She pushed the books from her chest, stood up, and stretched.
An unlikely Phoenix rising from the ash, she rejoiced.
She had never moved on her own before.
She sped through the black streets, somehow
seeing. There was not enough oxygen left to light a match,
cursed a hearty cockroach who scampered beside her.
In the distance she could make out a slightly charred Ken.
They ran into each other's arms, finally having the chance to live out
what was prior only in their imaginations. Barbie wished
for romance and a field of daisies or tall grasses.
Instead she heard hideous sirens, hinting
at further malfunctions. Barbie and Ken fled,
searching for a yellow sign—Fallout Shelter.
They hid behind sacks of flour and cans of baked beans,
hugging and fondling, without eggs or sperm,
without uterus or penis. Without tongues or breath, the two kissed
and vowed to protect each other forever. Without factories
or human children, Barbie and Ken were all each other had left.

Devon Nekoba
performer

Let me first say that it is an honor to be chosen to represent the wonderful 'ohana of actors that participated in *Aloha Shorts* over the years. I found the experience to be one of the most exhilarating, daunting, and fun experiences I've had as an actor . . . and yes, you heard that right, ACTOR . . . because Phyllis, Sammie, and Craig made sure we understood that we were chosen for our ability to bring these stories to life for people, sometimes with the author sitting ten feet away!

There was always an element of theater, because we had a live audience, and because we pretty much had to get it right the first time (although we would every so often go back and fix a word or two that may have gotten lost here or there). Then there was the acting component, because we worked with other actors at times, sometimes by ourselves, and characters always needed to be given a specific voice.

As an alumnus of Lisa Matsumoto's plays, and a fan of both Lee Cataluna and Lee Tonouchi, it was always great to throw out some Pidgin English in a piece, and I marveled at my fellow actors and their ability to bring these stories to life.

Aloha Shorts remains one of my favorite things I've done as an actor, and I hope everyone gets a chance to do something this special and representative of the Hawai'i arts and literature community. Mahalo, Phyllis, Sammie, and Craig, for working so hard to bring this program to life!

Toads
Darrell H.Y. Lum
from *Pass On, No Pass Back!*, first aired October 27, 2009

"So what you gonna be?" Barry went ask me.

"What *you* going be?" I went ask him back.

"I going be Zorro! Going be sharp man . . . my mahdah made me one cape and I going get one black hat and I went make one mask wit two eyeholes. I get one good stick fo use fo da sword. Going be sharp man. Shht, shht, shht!" Barry went make da Z for Zorro wit his hand. Den he went poke me wit his finger, "En garde! So what you going be?"

"I donno yet, I told you. I just was going use my mask, da one we made in school."

"Eh, sick dat. J'like da pumpkin we had to make out of da paper bag. Sick."

Halloween time we always gotta do da same ting. We gotta bring one big paper bag and stuff um wit newspaper and tie da top wit string and paint um orange and da stem green and make one scary black face wit hammajang teet. Ho, hard fo carry dat ting home, da paint all flake off da package and da flakes go on your clothes and your mahdah put um out in da living room fo little while, even aftah Halloween pau.

"Why no be Hopalong Cassady. Or maybe da Long Ranger. Dah-dah dunt, dah-dah dunt, dah-dah dunt dunt dunt . . . ."

"Hiyo, Silvah! Awaaay . . . ."

"I thought you was going be Long Ranger. Dat would be sharp. Or what about da horse, Silva. Wynette Silva."

"Shaddap. I no like girls with one moustache. Zorro going be good though."

"Yeah. What Jocks Full Loo going be?"

"Same. Everytime he like be one football player. And Na-na-nasubi said he like come with us."

"What, dat tilly?"

Na-na-nasubi was kinda tilly so could make him scared kinda easy. He could play jacks good though, even bettah than da girls. Especially da one you gotta do around-da-worlds and no can show teeth. And he was smart. Everybody wanted to copy his homework paper so no good tease him too much, bumbye he no let you copy.

Barry said, "Before he come wit us, he gotta go trick o treat at da haunted house."

"Da green house?"

"Yeah."

"Ho, man!"

"If he like come wit us, he gotta go dere first and if he make it, den he can come with us."

Had dis old green house on the way home from school, weeds all around, tall kine weeds and nobody next door 'cause was one Hawaiian Electric place with all the electric machinery and one wire fence all around and even had barbed wire on top. And on the other side of the haunted house was the dirt and gravel driveway wit the weeds so tall on the sides and in the middle only could walk where the tires went. And had toads all ovah in the grass, so even in the day, we only walked on the two dirt parts . . . even after the rain, when was muddy and had puddles, we walked only where the tires went 'cause once, we went walk little bit in the tall grass and the grass started moving and you could see um move because someting inside the tall grass went move and den stop and den move again. I went blast the place wit rocks and den all these toads started coming out of the grass. Hopping anykine way. J'like they was coming to get me. Ho, I went grab my school bag and make it! Barry said that his mother told him no touch toad bumbye you going get warts and anykine ooh-gee stuff. You going start to get bumps on top your skin and den your eyes going pop out, la dat. Bull liar I tink, yeah?

Spooky walk over dere, but me and Barry cut short by ovah dere everytime 'cause had one water pipe fo drink water and no mo old lady bother you about, "Get away from the water hose!" "Who told you you could use my water?" and "You better close the pipe good, now."

The house was all green peeling paint and was all closed up. All the doors was closed, but some windows was broken and could see inside one room. Was only empty, all dusty and stink air.

One time Barry went take my coin purse, the plastic kine that look like one football and when you squeeze um, look like one mouth opening. No worry, nevah have any money dat time. He was fussing around wit um. You know, making like he was eating my hand, my ear, my nose, la dat. Den he went swing um around on da chain and he was making um go faster and faster and went fly off his hand and go ovah the electrical fence.

"Shet, I going had it," I told him. "I going get it, stupid. Now what I going do?"

Barry said, "No worry, I help you get um. I going get one stick and we can hook um and get um back." So we was trying to get the purse back from behind the fence and we was doing pretty good. I could just get my hand between the fence and the post and I was reaching wit all my might. I couldn't even turn my head fo see; my eyes was shut so I could reach as far as can. Barry was telling me go dis way or dat way, hold it, hold it. And den Barry nevah say nutting fo long time and I finally went turn and open my eyes and had one big Bufo wit his throat all puffed up right next to my face. Barry nevah say nutting, he was so scared of da toad. He jes was looking at da toad and da toad was looking at him, side-eye, and was j'like he wanted fo get up and run away but he couldn't. I was scared too, but I wasn't as scared as Barry. I jes went tell, "Eh, nemmine da coin purse awready. We go."

I went tell Barry everytime I see one squashed toad on da road, dat it remind me of da Chinese herb man. I told him dat inside his shop get anykine dried up stuff . . . real animals, la dat. Jocks Full Loo said that probably even get some mummy heads and all shriveled up small pa-ke heads with eyeballs and nose hairs and bolo heads and warts and wrinkles and tough skin still yet warm, like one old wallet with some places worn smooth and some places all wrinkly. Barry nevah say too much about dat time and he jes went look at me like "ooh-gee" when I told him about the Chinese man, so I nevah say nutting aftah dat.

The electricity place had anykine signs: WARNING, KEEP OUT, HIGH VOLTAGE, KEEP AWAY. SEVERE ELECTRICAL SHOCK HAZARD. And always had one hum. Low hum. I liked dat place even though was little bit spooky wit all da signs la dat, but all da wires and the round tings wit da fins look like antennas to me. J'like Roy Rogers . . . I mean, Buck Rogers and da space ship and da alien guns. Once, I even saw one blue spark go "pak!" from one green antenna to da uddah one. And fo one second was all quiet. Nutting . . . no mo sound. Just da funny "tick" and "tack" of da metal. J'like was breathing, da machinery. Den went start up again. Spooky, da hum, da green machinery, da old green house, da green toads.

So had me and Barry, he was going be Zorro, and Jocks Full Loo, he was one football player. The helmet always so big dat Jocks Full had to walk around wit his head tilted back so dat he could see, uddahwise he gotta hold on to the face mask wit one hand and the football wit da uddah hand and den no mo hand fo hold his bag fo da candy. Sometimes he so stoopid sometimes. And Na-na-nasubi had one plastic suit wit one skeleton printed on top. His mahdah always buy him store-bought stuff. Barry went ask him, "Who you?" And Na-na-nasubi went say, "One sk . . . sk . . . skeleton." And Barry nevah catch and went tell, "You mean like Red Skeleton? He no look la dat . . . ." I had to laugh. Sometimes Barry smart. Sometimes he stupid. Sometimes no can tell.

Me, I was one shipwreck guy. Every year I one bust up shipwreck guy. My mahdah no buy me nutting; she no make me nutting. I gotta wear all da rag-bag stuff. I even rip um up so come more ugly and wind some old white rags around my head fo bandages and den get da Mercurochrome and make like get blood all on da bandages. Den I ask my bruddah use da matches and burn one old cork . . . Daddy had da corks all in one old cookie can. You burn um until da stuff come all black and you can paint your face wit um. My bruddah can make um look j'like you all bus up but still yet alive from one explosion.

We was walking to da green house already. Me and Barry, den Jocks Full Loo little bit behind 'cause he was having hard time wit his helmet and his football and his trick o treat bag. I told you, eh. And had Na-na-nasubi mo behind den dat.

"So what, we going let Na-na-nasubi come wit us or what?" Barry went tell real loud so dat Na-na-nasubi could hear. "He no can come wit us if he going be one tilly. I no like no tillies come wit us. Tillies no can go da haunted house."

"Na . . . na . . . naht. I . . . I . . . I naht!" Na-na-nasubi went tell.

We told Na-na-nasubi that if he wanted to be on our gang, he had to go trick or treat at the haunted house wit us. He had to go and say, "trick o treat" and he couldn't just say, "chrickochreat" real fast and den run away. He had to say um slow and wait until somebody came to the door and no worry, we stay backing him up. But if one big toad went come to da door, he had to spit on um before he came back by us.

We went walk all da way to da haunted house, me and Barry and Jocks Full. Na-na-nasubi kept getting more and more behind. Could tell he was getting scared. Wasn't dat scary. Wasn't dark or anyting. We had to wait fo him by the porch of da house.

"Okay, go trick o treat at da door. You gotta stay dere by yourself now. And when somebody come to da door, den you call us," Barry told him.

Barry went give us da signal and we went make like we was backing him up and Barry went crawl undah da house right undah da porch. As soon as Na-na-nasubi went knock, Jocks Full and me went hide in the tall grass. Na-na-nasubi was getting kinda hard time even saying "trick o treat."

"Tr . . . tr . . . tree . . ." And everytime he went knock on da door and say "trick o treat," Barry went bang one rock on da floor undah da house and make in one spooky voice, "Whaat? Whachulike? Who you?" Bang, bang, bang! And Na-na-nasubi went turn around and he nevah see us and da floor was going bang, bang, bang, and we was hiding and laughing until I went tink of da toads dat must stay inside da grass and the Chinese medicine man wit da dried up animals and da dead toads on da street and da grass started moving and da electrical place came quiet. No mo hum, j'like the blue spark time. So I went get up from my hiding place and Na-na-nasubi went see me and started fo come by us. And den we went hear Barry say, "Shet. Shet. I went touch one toad!"

He came out from undah da house holding out his hand. "I thought da toad was da rock. Shet. Aw, shet. I going get all ugly."

We wanted to go by him fo see if he was going get all hairy or someting, but j'like we nevah like go by him jes in case he touch us.

"We go some houses," I said and jes started walking. Had me and Na-na-nasubi and Jocks Full in front and Barry was walking kinda behind us, crying little bit and everytime saying, "Shet." We had to wait fo him while he went back to his house and wash real good and change his Zorro costume 'cause he said might have toad shet on top.

"Whachumean might have toad shet! You ever seen toad shet before?" I told him. "We jes go already. You gotta be Zorro! Gotta go shht, shht, shht."

"Yeah but, must be toads shet," Barry went tell. "So wait fo me!"

"Okay, okay. But I nevah seen no toad shet."

We all wanted to be first to hit one house and ring da doorbell and say, "Trick or treat" 'cause you like, da kine, make da guys dat open da door scared, eh? And if get good stuff and plenny uddah guys at da door, you can get some candy den go to da back of da bunch and wait and den get somemore.

So when Na-na-nasubi was first, he went get kinda excited and scared. When he come la dat, he no can talk. Come stuck da words. He no can make um come out. "Trr . . . trr . . . chrr . . . chrree . . . ah, shet!" Us guys we used to to it already. We no mind. Ass how he talk. You can feel um get stuck in his throat and j'like da words stay stuck in our throat too and we stay tinking: trick o treat, trick o treat, trick o treat. And everybody stay *tinking* um, but nobody stay saying um. And Na-na-nasubi stay all embarrassed and he just turn around to us and all of a sudden we all stay saying, "Trick o treat. Trick o treat. Trick o treat!" And Na-na-nasubi is saying um wit us . . . perfeck. He just needed to, j'like, warm up his voice; get um used to talking den it came out okay. Aftah dat he could say um good, "Trick o treat! Trick o treat!" everytime.

And aftah dat, we went call Barry "Toadshet."

A Day in da Life of a Java Junkie

Lisa Linn Kanae

from *Bamboo Ridge* Issue #77, first aired December 8, 2009

7:30 a.m.   I finally did it; I chrew my radio alarm clock out da window. It isn't dat I don't enjoy waking up with Michael W. Perry and Larry Price. Oh no. On da contrary. Dey just sound so annoyingly chipper every morning—in one Yuban-kine way. Dey probably had deah caffeine fix dis morning. Me? I still stay wondering how my dog wen cockroach my pillow. Rise and shine. Seize da day. It is imperative dat I greet my Mr. Coffee even before I attempt to empty my bladder.

7:45 a.m   I get fifteen minutes for haul my okole out da front door. I no more time for grind whole beans: gotta reach for da grounds dis morning—a noble sacrifice for a coffee connoisseur such as myself. What shall it be? Sumatra Roast? Guatemala Antigua? Chocolate Macadamia Nut? Medaglia D'oro Espresso. *Sì!* Authentic Italian style coffee. Hand selected beans dat are double roasted and ground for an unusually rich, aromatic, delicious cup of coffee. Gee, I feeling kinda Italian already. *Buon giorno. Per favore. Gràzie.*

As I pour hot coffee into my 20 oz. travel coffee mug, I suddenly hear my mother's voice.

"You like fibroids in your breasts? Your teeth going turn brown: your hair going turn gray. Caffeine is one diuretic, you know. You going dehydrate. Your skin going shrivel up. You going deplete all the vitamin B in your body. Is that what you want?"

No Ma, what I really want is hair on my chest. No worry. I going quit drinking coffee tomorrow. No bahdah me now. I gotta go work. *Ciao.*

9:00 a.m.   Ho cuz, my brain cells stay doing da bump! I'm feeling kind of incandescent dis morning. My senses are sharp; my nerves are steely. And praise da Lord, I can walk and chew gum. I not worried: I can kick caffeine whenevahs. It's easy. I do it all da time. In fact, according to my extensive research, Fridays is da best day for kick one caffeine habit, because on Saturday I can suffa from da shakes in da privacy of my own home. On Sunday I no need go church because I will have already seen eeda Jesus or Elvis. By Monday, I will have taken enough aspirin to kill one bamboocha laboratory rat. I going quit drinking coffee tomorrow. I will. It's just one matter of willpower.

1:00 p.m.   I wen tell dat pesky boss of mine dat I no can give blood to da Blood Bank dis afternoon. What? Give up my coffee break? I don't think so. I told my boss dat I have to operate one moving vehicle for go home. I not going give up my fifteen-minute cup of vending machine joe. Forget it. I realize dat plenny people look down on vending machine coffee. I like to tink dat I'm above dat. I like to tink dat I'm more righteous den all does pretentious Starbucks types who have made coffee drinking one elitist pastime. Granted, vending machine coffee kind of sucks. However, vending machine coffee represents da working class. I may not be one of da privileged, but at least I get da right amount of quarters.

6:00 p.m.   Starbucks Cafes are so disgusting. God, I hope nobody in here recognizes me. Look at deese people. So high maka maka. Dey make caffeine addiction look so trendy. Naturally, I no belong amongst deese types. I one salt-of-da-earth-kine addict. I not one Banana Republic–wearing, caramel macchiato–ordering, cell phone–answering, café carousa!

I feel weak.

Dis coffee smell so ono. I gotta order something, but I must blend in . . .

Excuse me. Barista, do you think that maybe you could take my order now, I've been standing here, like, forever, thank you very much. Give me a skinny triple latte. Light foam. Yes, leave a little room on the top for some two per cent. Oh OK. A shot of hazelnut sounds, like, perfect. Not too much now. Lycra jersey miniskirts can be so unforgiving. Oh, puh-shaw. Pour more than that. Ohmygaw!

WATCHOO MEAN, DECAF?

Eh, Brah. I look like one decaf to you? I don't tink so. I like diesel in my coffee. Neva mind da chocolate dust. Only panties like chocolate sprinkled on top deah foam.

2:00 a.m.   I NO CAN SLEEP! All dis tossing and turning is torture. Gunfunnit Mrs. Olson! You and your charming European accent. No make like you da sweet little immigrant lady next door. Undahneat dat frumpy housecoat and support hose lives a ruthless java pusher. I know dat she one cohort of Juan Valdez. I know what his donkey staying smuggling out of da coffee fields, and it ain't from Kona.

I no can sleep.

Naturally, dis all my parents' fault. Dey da ones started every morning wit one hot pot of Folgers. Coffee after breakfast, coffee after lunch, coffee after dinna . . . down to da last drop. When I was small I was force for walk down supermarket aisles lined wit big coffee tins. Da coffee cans jeered, made fun of my desire to drink sissy sodas and Kool-Aid. For Chrissakes, I wen scream, I just one kid. But dey neva care. Dey wen push whateva stash dey had in my face. First was dat seemingly benevolent Ovaltine. Da bugga was smooth. Den dat slut, Miss Swiss Hot Cocoa Mix, she wen flaunt her just-add-water-and-stir packages all ova da store. Den, I started hanging wit da Nestle's Cocoa Rabbit. I did it all—powders, syrups, instant, house blend. On real bad days, I did a line of Sanka. By dat time I was fifteen years old, I was hanging out at da King's Bakery Coffee Shop counter scamming for free refills.

I am clearly a victim of a society dat has institutionalized caffeine dependency. How can one impressionable youth not be tempted by da bean, when da bean is all dat child has eva known. It's time to stop da jitters, da coffee-breath, da constipation.

Braddas and sistas, decolonize your kitchens! Drink Water! Tink about da innocent childrens who already know da difference between one breve and one Americano.

Quit drinking coffee—tomorrow.

Did I mention dat I smoke?

Oz Kalani, Personal Trainer

Cedric Yamanaka

from *The Best of HONOLULU Fiction*, first aired November 23, 2010

Oz Kalani was the kind of person who believed a life could be created, transformed, defined by a single moment. This was his.

Hawaii Five-O. Episode Number 21. "Aloha Means Goodbye." A pyromaniac extortionist threatens to set the entire island on fire unless he is given a priceless feather cape once worn by ancient ali'i, now under lock-and-key at the Bishop Museum. Remember that episode? There's the scene where a Lincoln Continental explodes on a Chinatown street. The extortionist guy ducks down an alley. Steve McGarrett, immaculate in a dark suit and tie, gives chase.

"Which way did he go, bruddah?" McGarrett asks a young taxi driver.

"Dat way," says the young taxi driver, pointing towards Diamond Head. He is wearing a blue Aloha shirt and a straw hat.

McGarrett, without another word, runs after the extortionist.

That young taxi driver was none other than the hero of our story, Oz Kalani. And *Hawaii Five-O*, Episode 21, was Oz Kalani's television debut.

From the show themed "Hawaii Five-O," *Aloha Shorts* host and author Cedric Yamanaka flanked by readers of his work Moses Goods III (left) and Aito Simpson Steele.

"Dis is it, boys!" I remember an excited Oz Kalani saying the night the episode aired. We watched the show in the living room of his Kuhio Park Terrace one-bedroom apartment. "Dis is Da One . . . ."

"Da what?" one of us asked, confused.

"Da One!" said Oz Kalani, wearing a puka-shell necklace and Hang Ten T-shirt. "Da Big One!"

"Da Big What?" someone said, still confused.

That's when Oz Kalani leaned over and told us his philosophy on life.

"Lissen," he said, sighing and sounding slightly exasperated. "I going only say dis once. In every person's life, deah comes a moment wheah his life can change forevahs. One chance. Dis *Hawaii Five-O* ting, dis is it. My ticket out of heah. Oz Kalani is a new man."

Days after *Hawaii Five-O*'s Episode 21 was aired, CBS Television and the Diamond Head studio where the show was taped were inundated with hundreds of telephone calls asking about the young taxi driver. Who was he? When would we see more of him? How, you may be asking yourself, would your humble narrator know the inner workings of a major television production? How would he know that producers and executives were barraged with dozens of questions about Oz Kalani? I know, dear friends, because I made the majority of these inquiries. At Oz's request.

"Eh, Oz!" someone said, that day me and several of Oz's closest friends worked the phones like a bunch of crazed telethon volunteers. "You can do me one favor, or what? You can get me Jack Lord's autograph?"

"Shoots," said Oz Kalani.

"And ask em how he keep his hair so nice. Da thing nevah get messy, you notice dat? And even when da thing get little bit messy, like if da wind blow 'em around, da buggah still look shaka. You notice dat? Kinda like Elvis. Oh and ask em if can borrow dat big, black Cadillac of his to drive around. I get one date with Sassy Nancy next week. Dat car would impress da pants off her . . ."

"I see what I can do," said Oz Kalani.

Believe it or not, Oz Kalani's plan worked. He had created the illusion of public demand. He was asked to do another *Hawaii Five-O*. Episode 32. "Beretania Street is a One-Way Street, Ewa Bound." Oz Kalani is a down-on-his-luck boxer looking for quick cash. He joins an Asian heroin ring led by the international criminal Wo Fat. You remember the menacing Wo Fat? Bald head, thin moustache. Wo Fat's first order to Oz is, indeed, an evil one. Place poisonous blowfish meat on the governor's inaugural dinner plate. Oz's conscience, however, gets the best of him and he dutifully climbs the steps up to 'Iolani Palace and reports the vile scheme to McGarrett.

In the end, McGarrett and yes, Oz Kalani, capture Wo Fat at the old Oceania Floating Restaurant in Honolulu Harbor.

"I'll get you, McGarrett," says Wo Fat perfectly sinister.

"Book em, Danno," says McGarrett, unruffled.

"Ho, awesome!" we said, once again watching the broadcast in the living room of Oz Kalani's Kuhio Park Terrace one-bedroom apartment. We cheered and clapped and popped open a bottle of Cold Duck.

"Dis is Big," said Oz Kalani, flushed and triumphant. "Dis is Da Big One!"

"No forget us, when you famous, ah?" someone said, maybe me.

"No worry," said Oz Kalani, with a wink that was somehow, both reassuring and confident at the same time. "I going buy one big mansion and we going sit by the pool, eat poke and drink beer . . ."

"Legend," someone said.

"Giant," another said.

"King," still a third said.

Everyone wanted to be like Oz Kalani. Not just because he was on *Hawaii Five-O*. Ever since we were kids, growing up in Kalihi, Oz Kalani was one handsome buggah. Tall, square chin, white teeth, body tanned from years of surfing off Canoes and Kaisers, brown eyes sweet as chocolate-covered macadamia nuts. But it wasn't simply because of his drive, his desire. Unlike most of us, he knew exactly what he wanted to do with himself. He knew exactly where he wanted to go.

Let me make the record clear, ladies and gentlemen. Oz Kalani was no overnight success. Whatever triumphs life handed him, he earned through years of hard work, focus, and dedication. We all saw it. Even in the very early days at Kapalama Elementary School.

While the rest of us in the fourth grade played kickball and rode skateboard at Uluwatus, Oz Kalani scripted a ghost story. One day, during class, he acted it out for us. I don't remember much about the performance except it was supposed to occur in a graveyard and once or twice, he turned off the lights and screamed. The lunch bell rang during Oz's play, I remember, but nobody moved from their seats. The ultimate compliment.

As the years went by, Oz nurtured his love for the stage. He played Brutus in a Farrington High School production of Shakespeare's *Julius Caesar*. Caesar was being played by our dork valedictorian and in the scene where Brutus stabs Caesar to death, everyone in the audience cheered and chanted Oz's name. "Oz-zie! Oz-zie! Oz-zie!"

At the University of Hawai'i, Oz Kalani was Tony in *West Side Story*. He was the Man of La Mancha, the King in *The King and I*, Jesus in *Jesus Christ Superstar*.

But it was television that excited Oz Kalani most, and one show in particular.

"I gotta get on *Hawaii Five-O*," he told me one day.

That was the one thing we had in common. We were both big fans of *Hawaii Five-O*. I still am. I've watched every episode, remembered all the plots, tracked the numerous guest appearances by local celebrities. I'm a walking *Hawaii Five-O* encyclopedia.

Anyway, Oz Kalani submitted dozens of photographs and cover letters to *Hawaii Five-O* executives and one glorious day, he was called in to do a reading. The rest, as they say, is history.

Now, after his first two *Hawaii Five-O* appearances, Oz Kalani's future looked as bright as the white shoes and polyester pants Steve McGarrett sometimes wore. Rumors about Oz were everywhere. The producers at *Hawaii Five-O* appreciated Oz Kalani's talent so much, they planned to offer him a role on the series as a regular. Right up there with Danno, Kono, and Chin Ho.

"Da deal is dis," Oz confided. "Me and McGarrett, we going be partners. Like Batman and Robin . . ."

Another rumor circulating around Kalihi revealed that some big-time Hollywood producer vacationing on Maui saw Oz Kalani on *Hawaii Five-O* and wanted him to be the lead in a film biography about King Kamehameha the Great.

Oz Kalani hired himself a mainland agent. The agent got him a role as an extra when the *Brady Bunch* came to town. The agent also got him a cameo on *Charlie's Angels*, the two-parter when the girls visited the islands.

Now if life was fair, Oz Kalani would have become famous, a household name, a star of stage and screen, a legend. You'd have seen him thanking God, his agent, and his family at the Academy Awards, holding up the golden Oscar statue after winning Best Actor. You'd have seen his picture on the covers of *Time, Newsweek, Life, People, Esquire,* and *Rolling Stone*. You'd have seen film clips of him on the news, walking hand-in-hand with beautiful starlets in exotic locations. In a tuxedo in Cannes. Climbing out of a limo in Hong Kong. Dining out in a trendy Manhattan bistro. You'd have seen him as the grand marshal of parades. You'd have seen him sing "The Star-Spangled Banner" before the Super Bowl. You'd have seen his star on the Hollywood Walk of Fame.

If life was fair.

Alas, Oz Kalani was never asked to be a regular on *Hawaii Five-O*. He would not play Kamehameha on the big screen. And after a while, the phone stopped ringing and the offers stopped coming. The letters and photographs he sent out in the mail returned unopened. The well appeared to be running dry.

"What happened to yoah agent?" some asked.

"He trying," said Oz. "He say no worry."

Now, no one loved Oz Kalani more than Yours Truly. But I must confess to you that during this dark and frightening period in his life, Oz Kalani became a royal pain in the you-know-where. Take going to the movies, for example.

"You call dat acting?" I remember him whispering during a feature at the Cinerama one night. "I can do bettah dan dat clown . . ." He memorized lines during the movie, leaned over to me, and recited them. "How's dat? Good, ah? Bettah dan dat bastard, ah? Da buggah getting all kind awards. He one millionaire. Wahines all ovah da place. Jeez . . ."

Aloha Shorts host Cedric Yamanaka is interrogated by "private eye" Derek Ferrar (of Hamajang) during an interlude in the show themed "Hawaii Five-O"

When we saw the *Godfather*, Oz Kalani said he could give shooting lessons to the Corleone family.

"But dey all gangsters," I said. "Dey awready know how shoot . . ."

"You just no undahstand da acting business," said Oz, rolling his eyes.

During *Jaws*, Oz wanted to help Quint, Brodie, and Hooper kill the great white shark.

"I come from a long line of fishermans," he said. "If I was on dat sorry ass boat, I'd shove my tree prong spear right into dat shark's eye. Dead meat, brah . . . ."

Oz wanted to be the first Hawaiian in space after watching *Star Wars* and *E.T.*

"Who's dis Dart Vadah clown?" said Oz Kalani. "You think he scare me? He's nothing. One panty. Half da boys at K.P.T. could knock him out . . . ."

And when we saw *Rocky*, Oz Kalani wanted to beef the Italian Stallion. "I can be the scrapping Hawaiian," he said. "I'd give dat bruddah dirty lickings . . . ."

Yes, sadly, Oz Kalani was becoming angry and disgruntled. But he had a point.

"Deah's no good scripts foah us local guys," he'd always say. "No good parts. You know dat. I know dat. My useless agent know dat. And you know why dat is? Because da big wig mainland executives, dey no care about Hawai'i. Dey come heah, go Waikīkī Beach and Pearl Harbor. But dey no really care about da Hawaiian peoples . . . ."

Sadly, Oz Kalani and I started drifting apart. I'm not sure why. It didn't happen in a day. It was a gradual thing. We just saw less and less of each other. Before I knew it, a year had passed. Then two. Then three. One day, I called his home. A recorded voice said she was sorry but I have reached a number that was vacant and no longer in service. I asked around. No one seemed to know what happened to Oz Kalani. It was as if he had disappeared from the of the Earth.

As for me, fate led me down the improbable path of Animal Medicine. I became, of all things, a veterinarian. One day, I treated a Doberman afflicted with bad breath. On top of my usual fee, the Doberman's grateful owner gave me a lifetime membership to the Ikaika Fitness Center.

I was not what you'd call a health freak. I readily admit I could have gotten a little more exercise, maybe trimmed a pound or two off the midsection. And while a number of friends and acquaintances had turned to tofu, stir fry, and salads, I clung to the old favorites like New York steaks, chili burgers, and kalbi ribs. And while others warned me about the health risks, I heartily enjoyed cups of strong coffee, a Chivas Regal after a particularly hard day, and an occasional Cuban cigar.

Still, I decided to check out the Ikaika Fitness Center and, yes, I was impressed. Heated pools, saunas, Jacuzzis, racquetball courts, basketball courts, rows and rows of exercise bicycles and Stairmasters, dozens of fitness machines and free weights.

My first day there, I saw a beautiful girl in skintight leotards standing in front of a mirror curling tiny dumbbells, one in each hand.

"Very good, sweetie," said a huge guy next to her. Obviously an instructor. And then it hit me. The pecs were bigger, the quads more expansive, the biceps and triceps more defined but—of course—the instructor was none other than my dear, long-lost friend, Oz Kalani. But I had to be sure.

"Excuse me," I said, tapping the instructor on a massive and very hard shoulder.

"Just a second," he said, not turning around." You wanna work out? Call me."
He handed me a business card.

Oz Kalani, Personal Trainer

"Oz," I said. "It's me."

He turned around and when he finally realized who I was, his eyes opened real wide and he hugged me. After the girl's workout was finished, Oz invited me to the lounge on the first floor of the gym. The Ikaika Bar. I was looking forward to a beer. Oz Kalani ordered two zucchini and broccoli shakes. The guy gave it to him for free. That was no surprise. An autographed photograph of none other than Oz Kalani—pumped and smiling—hung on the wall, behind the cash register.

"Damn, it's good to see you," said Oz, as we sat on a terrace overlooking a Jacuzzi. He sized up my body in that unique way guys who lift a lot of weights like to size up other people's bodies. "So what you doing with yoah life now?"

"Me?" I said, touched by his interest, to be honest with you, "I'm a veterinarian."

"Oh yeah?" said Oz, very impressed. "Awesome, brah! Whoo, I admire you guys! So what? You no eat meat? How about chicken?"

"No, no," I corrected. "I'm a *veterinarian*. Not vegetarian. *Veterinarian*."

"Oh," said Oz, nodding. "But what about seafood? Fish and stuff . . . ."

"No," I persisted. "You see . . . ."

"Eh," said Oz, apparently tired of the subject. "I'm glad you're working out. Shape dat body of yoahs. Sculpt it da way one artist carves art out of one slab of marble . . . ."

"Dis is my first day," I said.

"It's so easy," said Oz Kalani. "Keeping fit. Dis is da only body you'll evah have. You bettah take care of it . . . ."

Oz Kalani explained how he was a personal trainer, working out one-on-one with politicians, celebrities, and businessmen.

"Uh," I ventured. "What happened to yoah acting career?"

"Oh dat?" said Oz, waving at two girls daintily dipping their toes in the Jacuzzi. "You've heard dose stories about some actor who worked as one waiter or one gas station attendant. Den one day, he's what-you-call discovered? Das what I'm doing. Only ting, I one personal trainer. I just passing time, waiting for da call to come. Da Big One. Den boom, my life going change. Das what my agent in Los Angeles says. He tell me, 'Be patient. Things are gonna happen.' And I believe him . . . ."

During the next several weeks, I visited the Ikaika Fitness Center every Monday, Wednesday, and Friday after work. Oz Kalani was always there. As I curled, pressed, squatted, and benched, I watched Oz assist nubile lasses as they stretched their hamstrings and looked lovingly in his eyes. I watched him cheer on sweaty, out-of-shape executives struggling on exercise bicycles. And I watched Oz diligently take pencil to clipboard as he charted the weight training progress of young college students hoping to impress girls in Hamilton Library with the size of their shoulders and chests.

Oz had a fast, breathless, machine gun–like way of dishing out encouragement. *C'mon!Youcandoit!Pushpushpush!* And all the while, he wore a tight polo shirt—with the handsome Ikaika Fitness Center emblem, available for $29.95 at the front desk— shorts, Nikes, and shades hanging down from a string around his neck. Sometimes— on bad hair days, he explained—he wore a baseball cap sporting the insignia of a winning athletic team or the logo of a successful designer footwear manufacturer.

One day, though, Oz wore something new. Something I hadn't seen in ages. He wore the look of hope, a blissful sleepwalker enjoying the greatest dream of his life. And that afternoon, over watercress smoothies and no-fat, no-cholesterol energy bars, I heard Oz Kalani's familiar refrain.

"Dis is Da Big One," he said.

"Da what?" I said, not sure I'd heard correctly.

"Da Big One," he repeated. "Remembah how I used to say one moment can change da course of yoah entire life?"

"Yeah," I said, the understatement of my life.

"A producer guy just offered me my own exercise show. Can you believe dat? We start shooting tomorrow. I want you to be in my first show. You going stand right next to me. Stretching, doing jumping jacks, lunges, da works . . . ."

"Who's dis producer guy?"

"One of da students in my Tuesday, Thursday aerobics class. Dey call him Da Kid. He said we going start locally. But who knows wheah dis going lead? Maybe I can go national, have my own exercise videos. Den some big time buggah going discover me. My dreams going come true . . . ."

"Da Kid?" I said.

"Yeah," he said, with a wink that reminded me of the old, confident Oz Kalani I used to know. "You know dese Hollywood guys. Dey give each othah all kind funny nicknames."

I have to admit. I was pretty excited that night. I couldn't eat well. I hardly slept. After all, unlike the extremely photogenic Oz Kalani, I had never been on TV before. How much mousse should I put in my hair? Would I sweat too much?

Words can't describe the surprise waiting for me the next day when Oz Kalani took me to the set of his exercise show. Maybe I was naïve. I was expecting us to tape at a beach or the grounds of a lush resort. Instead, Oz Kalani drove me to the employees' parking lot at the Ala Moana Shopping Center.

"Dis seems like a weird place to tape one exercise show," I said.

"You always so skeptical," said Oz Kalani, slightly annoyed. "Look at all the exercise shows on TV. Dey eithah working out in some fancy studio, or at some nice beach or golf course. Da Kid, he sharp. He like us be different . . . ."

"Whatevahs," I said, shrugging.

And, yes, words can't adequately describe the surprise when Oz Kalani introduced me to the big-time producer named Da Kid. Instead of some forty-something-year-old executive type with dark glasses and a pipe, I wound up shaking hands with, well, a kid. A sixteen-year-old stock clerk on his lunch break from an Ala Moana store.

"Are you Da Kid?" I said.

"Yes," said Da Kid.

"We going shoot Oz Kalani's exercise show in one parking lot?"

"Yep," said Da Kid. "And we gotta hurry up. I only get twenty minutes befoah I gotta go back work."

Oz took off his warm-up jacket, revealing skintight bike shorts as black and glossy as Steve McGarrett's hair. Da Kid positioned Oz and me just slightly left of a Toyota Tercel and an Acura.

"If you like," said Oz Kalani, "I can sing, too. I get one good voice. I could have done duets with Frank Sinatra. I could've been da Fifth Beatle. Or you rather hear my Elvis?"

Da Kid whipped out one of those home video cameras you use at surprise birthday parties and baby luaus and Oz took us through his workout regime. A group of onlookers slowly gathered, making me quite self-conscious, as you can imagine. We got through some stretching and light aerobics when disaster struck. Several burly security guards informed us that we were on private property and just as quickly, kicked us off the aforementioned private property. Tears streamed down my face.

"Eh," said Oz Kalani, putting a consoling arm around me. "No cry for me, pal. I going be all right . . . ." I didn't have the heart to tell Oz that somehow my cursed mousse had mixed with my sweat and run into my burning eyes. "I always thought my destiny was to be somebody," said Oz, watching a Nissan Pathfinder squeeze into a parking stall clearly labeled "compact." "I always thought I was going do Big Tings. Put Hawai'i on da map. Now, foah da first time in my life, I not so sure. Maybe I been wrong all dis time . . . ."

Oz Kalani was not at the Ikaika Fitness Center the next day. Nor did he make an appearance the next day. Or the next day. It was as if, once again, Oz Kalani had disappeared from the face of the Earth. For a while, rumors about Oz Kalani circulated among the members of the Ikaika Fitness Center. He had received an offer to serve as Chief Trainer at the exclusive—and rival—Hawai'i Club. Others said he was in Japan, personal therapist to sumo wrestlers. Still others said he was in Hollywood, signing a contract to star in an action thriller to be shot on location in Kaka'ako.

Recently, I was at Ikaika Fitness Center and there—before my very eyes—Oz Kalani made his triumphant return. Sort of. Actually, they were running an old rerun of *Hawaii Five-O* on the TV. And there was a much younger Oz Kalani, with so much hope and promise written on his eager face, pointing out the way a mad bomber had run to Steve McGarrett. I wanted so bad to hear Oz Kalani's voice one more time, but the clanking of the weights in the Ikaika Fitness Center drowned him out, kinda like the way you lose track of sound when you stick your head underwater.

Too Smart to Slow Down
A one-roach play in one act

Lanning C. Lee

from *Bamboo Ridge* Issue #52, first aired September 1, 2009

Scene: An aging cockroach, his long wings showing the wear of small cracks and a dulling luster, stands outside the screen door of a house in Honolulu. The stage is dimly lit, suggesting the nearly complete darkness of night—that time of night when humans have gone to sleep and roaches move about with the kind of freedom that they can never enjoy during daylight hours. Still, there are always risks for roaches, even in the dead of night. But this particular roach, called "Old McGann" by the million generations of cockroaches born after him, has lived long because he has learned from the fatal mistakes of others. Old McGann is as streetwise as any roach you will ever encounter.

Hungry. Always hungry.
Feel it feel it. Sniff it sniff it.
Under the door. Push push push push push.
Check left. Check right. Check up. Check down.
Walk walk walk walk walk. Walk walk walk walk walk.
Step on a crack, break your mother's back.
Oops, sorry, Mom. Oops, sorry, Mom. Oops, sorry, Mom.
      Oops, sorry, Mom. Oops, sorry, Mom. Oops, sorry, Mom . . .
      wherever you are.
Check left. Check right. Check up. Check down.
Walk walk walk walk walk. Walk walk walk walk walk.

Object.
Sniff it sniff it. Rubber object.
Sniff it sniff it. Two rubber objects.
Feel it feel it. Slippers. Unoccupied.
Sniff it sniff it. What a mess. All these guts. Must have known him.

Walk walk walk walk walk. Walk walk walk walk walk.
Obstruction.
Feel it feel it. Feel it feel it.
Concrete step.
Up, walk up, walk up, walk up. Up! Stop.
Clean myself?

Yes.
Suck suck lick. Suck suck lick.
That's enough.
Walk walk walk walk walk.
Sniff it sniff it. Feel it feel it.
Dog dish.

Up, walk up, walk upsidedown, walk upsidedown, walk up, walk up. Up!
Feel it feel it.
Check left, check right—

Hey George, how's it going? Long time no see.
Who are all these new kids?
All yours?
Congratulations.
Cigar? Sure, thanks. Mmmm, bubblegum.
Chew chew chew chew chew. Chew chew chew chew chew.

How's the Missus? Recovered yet?
Dead, huh? How long?
One hour? Sprayed?
Slippered. Too bad. Thought I smelled her over there.

Check left. Check right. Check up. Check down.

Brought 'um to the bowl, huh? Feeding frenzy.
Wanted McDonald's! Kids these days. Better get used to it. Dog food's the best.

Check left. Check right. Check up. Check down.

Seen Ed?
Dead, huh? How?
Slippered.
Seen Bob?
Dead, huh? How?
Slippered.
Seen John?
Dead, huh?
Seen Joe?

Ron?
Kimo?
Ralph?
All slippered! Too bad.
Hour ago? Too bad. Smelled 'um all.

Check left. Check right. Check up. Check down.

These kids—name 'um yet?
Junior! *All* Juniors?
Oh. Junior-One, Junior-Two—good idea. Let 'um pick their own names,
    if they grow up.
Time to eat, George. See ya 'round.
Down, slide down, slide down. Down!
Feel it feel it. Sniff it sniff it.

Ah, Purina. My favorite. Nice chunks.

Munch munch munch munch munch.
Munch munch munch munch munch.

Eh kid. You, Junior! Get your feelers outta my face. And clean the crumbs off
    those things, would yah!
Jeez, what a slob.
Don't know how to do it! Whatayah mean you don't know how to do it?
Some father. Some training.
Okay, listen.
Bend it down. Bend it. Not both of 'um. One at a time.
Now stick it in your mouth. That's it. Suck it. Pull it through while you suck it.
    That's it.
Now you got it, kid.
So beat it.
And by the way, ingrate, you're welcome!

Munch munch munch munch munch.
Munch munch munch . . . munch . . . mun . . .
Stop! Feel it feel it.
Check left . . . munch . . . check right . . . munch . . . check—

The jingle . . . that bouncing. Vibrations. The jingle chain jingle chain—

FIDO RAID! FIDO RAID!

George!
Get your kids to the bottom of the bowl!
George?
Listen up! Everybody dig to the bottom of the bowl!

Dig down dig down dig down dig down.

Hug the plastic!

That mouth like a cave and those grinding white fangs. Juniors being sucked up like
     whipped cream and chocolate sauce.
Sometimes I think Fido likes us more than his nuggets.

Jingle chain jingle chain getting softer. Vibrations fainter.

Up. Dig up, dig u—Jeez! Must have been hungry. Clean myself off.

Suck suck lick. Suck suck lick.

Up, walk up, slide down, walk up, walk up, slide down, walk up. Up! They're all
     gone? Where's George?

Check left. Check right. Check up. Check—
Oh, George!
Down, walk down, walk down, walk upsidedown, walk upsidedown, walk down.
Floor.

Sniff it sniff it. Feel it feel it.
George! Jeez, George. Two feelers, half a head, one leg.
Too bad. No one left. Just me.

Water. I want water.
Dog dish? Uh uh.
Sink? Too high.
Dishwasher? Maybe.

Check left. Check right. Check up. Check down.
Dishwasher? Yes.
Walk walk walk walk walk. Walk walk . . . walk . . . walk . . .

Vibrations. Slipper steps. Getting louder.

Ahhhhh! Bright light! Blinding!

SLIPPER RAID! SLIPPER RAID!

Dishwasher! Dishwasher!
Run run run run run.

Slipper slap whoosh wind.
Run run run run run.
Slipper slap whoosh wind.
Slide, baby, slide.
Slipper slap whoosh wind.

Push push squeeze. Push push squeeze.

Darkness breathe. Darkness breathe. Darkness breathe. Darkness breathe.

Check left. Check right. Check up. Check down.
Clean myself?
Not now.
Object.
Sniff it sniff it. Feel it feel it.
Wheel? . . . Wheel? Rolling wheel! Bright light! Blinding!

Slipper slap whoosh wind.
Run run run run run.
Slipper slap whoosh wind.
Fly, baby, fly!

Upside down. Ceiling.
Clean myself?
Not now.
Walk walk walk walk walk.

Look for darkness.
Walk walk walk walk walk.

Ahhh! [cough] Death cloud.
Door! Door!
Run run run run run. [cough]
Don't breathe.
Run [cough] run [cough] run. [cough]
Run down, run down. Down!
Push push squeeze. [cough] Push push squeeze.
Out the door.
Darkness.

Fly fly. [cough]
Fly fly. [cough]
Land. [cough]

Sniff it sniff it. Feel it feel it.
Tree trunk. Mossy.
Breathe.
[Cough]
Breathe.
[Cough]
Breathe.
Clean myself?
Not now.
Water.
Wash it off.
Stream? No.
Fish pond? Maybe.
[Cough]
Breathe.
[Cough]
Breathe . . .
Breathe . . .
Breathe . . .

Featured musical guests Jon Osorio (left)
and Duncan Kamakana Osorio

HAWAIIAN WRITERS

It was Sunday night, August 2, 2009—our eleventh taping. We were getting the hang of how to produce these events, and we'd even begun to attract quite a following. On this particular evening, however, there was an added something in the air—a tension, a palpable electricity. We had announced that all our readings would be by Hawaiian writers. Our special musical guest was renowned Hawaiian singer/songwriter/ scholar/activist Jon Osorio. His sidemen were his son and daughter, Duncan and Jamaica Osorio, and Tim Sprowls. In a departure from our usual format, the musicians would remain on stage throughout, interjecting their songs at specific times. The actors were like racehorses, panting and pawing at the starting gate. The audience was ready for something extraordinary.

And we were off. First with stories of small kid time, followed by the Osorios' rendition of Keola and Kapono Beamer's "Only Good Times." Then the amazing performance of "'Au 'A 'Ia," which Nara Cardenas narrated while playing a contrapuntal hula rhythm on her sternum, followed by a performance of the Hawaiian Renaissance anthem "Hawaiian Soul," written by Jon Osorio and Randy Borden. The show recorded after the intermission started with a lighter tone, led by Ginger Gohier's city girl who comes to understand "Bearing the Light." But we closed with Puanani Burgess's description of an excursion to and through the history inhabiting 'Iolani Palace in her poem "Hawai'i Pono'i," followed by "Kaulana Nā Pua" with a stunning, contemporary translation.

Wish you could have been there.

Bearing the Light
N. Keonaona (Aea) Russell
from Mālama: Hawaiian Land and Water, first aired November 17, 2009

Everywhere—black. The ocean and sand are without color except for where we stand. We move forward, water lapping at our knees and rolling over exposed rock. I glance up. Ahh, more light—real light, a million white eyes that never blink. Even at day. For whatever I am doing here, I ask mercy of the night.

Glenn raises a hand and whispers, "Come closer, Babe. I think I see something. 'Kay holdit. That's good."

I sway back and forth, hoping the wana and sharp coral won't cut through the tattered soles of my Nikes. I wiggle my toes, I wiggle my heels. Sand. I stare at my bare legs and arms. Goosebumps.

"Hold still," Glenn says. He raises his spear and plunges it downward like Thor throwing a lightning bolt.

I feel—rather than hear—a crunch near my foot. I take two shaky steps back, wave the net and snarl, "You almost hit my foot, you just missed it by—"

"Awright!" Glenn cries. He laughs as he stares past the widening ripples. "I got it! Wooooooo, tako and poi tomorrow. Tako and poi!" He lifts the spear then frowns at the brown lump impaled on it.

"What *is* that stuff, Glenn? Man, it's oozing blood."

"Watchit," my boyfriend says. He points to my hands. "Don't drop it. Don't get it wet."

"I know, I know." I raise the lantern past my head and our shadows lengthen.

Glenn slides the shriveled thing from his spear. "Sea cucumber," he mutters, tossing it past the circle of light. "C'mon, let's go further out."

I'd rather go further in. Like back to the dry Subaru, back to my warm apartment, back to a hot shower. Back in a place with lamps, and a stereo, and a pair of sweat pants. Instead, I walk beside Glenn and try not to bang my knees against the rocks.

My hair was already curled, and I was ironing a dress when Glenn phoned earlier this evening. He was supposed to take me to Spats, but he said that according to his tide calendar (Damn, I thought, I *knew* I shouldn't have given it to him for Christmas)—according to the calendar, tonight was a good night for torch fishing and would I mind if we did that instead of going to Spats. "We'll celebrate your birthday tomorrow," he said.

More than anything I wanted to say, "No way, Glenn. I ain't into sloshing after morays." But he was saying something about "perfect conditions," and how all I'd do was hold the light and maybe a net, and how I'd get the hang of it because it wasn't that hard. That's what he said.

Well, whatever this Coleman burns, it's giving me a headache. And my eyes hurt, and what's these pointy things that keep jabbing my legs? We've probably been here for at least an hour. Maybe if we head back to shore now we can make it to Spats. "Glenn? Hey Glenn—what time izzit?"

He straightens from a hunched position and squints. "What? What were you saying?"

I tap my wrist. "Time?"

He glances at his watch. "Little after nine. We been here almost twenty minutes. Let's go further out and walk parallel to shore. There's more people coming."

About a hundred yards to the left, a light seems to be approaching. Three people (including a child) are clustered around it. Sounds like they're laughing, or singing, or telling jokes. ("Knock knock." "Who's there?" . . .) Maybe they're a family. Or neighbors, or casual acquaintances. Maybe it doesn't matter. Some things don't when you're having fun. Whatever that is.

The shore is . . . it is . . . I glance left, right, left . . . the shore is . . . there. That must be it where the irregular string of lights are. Doesn't Glenn realize how far we've walked? (Walked? Ha! More like stumbled.) I'm not accustomed to sinking from knee-high to chest-deep water within a matter of one or two steps. Tricky, tricky the depth of these holes. Six inches equals one foot.

Fluorescent shrimp eyes, pairs of orange beads staring from holes I'd rather not poke. Kind of reminds me of Christmas, those eyes.

God, the stillness!

Could this really be the same beach where sunbathers and families congregate during the day? What happens to the jabber when the sun sets? Where are the swaggering hardbodies, the confident lifeguards, and the intense frisbee-flingers?

This cubic night and acres of silent, ancient ocean have metamorphosized us. Glenn and I, tentative intruders. The flip side of haughtiness—humility.

I carry the lantern in the crook of my arm, hugging it to my body. Friendly heat, warm eye. I think of the empty plastic bag in Glenn's backpack. He wants to catch an eel, some weke, trumpet fish, tako, *anything*—he says. As long as it's something.

Earlier, he paused in mid-step, lowered his face to the water. "Bring the light real close," he whispered. "I think it's an eel. Looks like some kind of dark eel against the sand there."

He plunged the spear forward (THOOMP) and his eyes widened. Happy green eyes. "It hardly moved. I got it, I got it!"

"Ha!" I said when he lifted his catch. "Some eel. From the Schwinn family, I suppose."

He pulled the inner tube off the prongs and shrugged. "Can't see everything clearly without perfect light."

We stumble on. I learn to dig the toe of my shoes into small holes, press my foot over the contours of the rocks. I slip once or twice, landing on my okole without dunking the lantern. "Good job," Glenn says. "You're getting the hang of it."

I ask him about the silvery-blue fish that keep poking my legs, and what're these things skimming over the water. "Needlefish," Glenn says. "They're okay. Won't gore through your legs."

He swishes the net back and forth, back and forth. Sometimes he scoops up rocks, bottles, palm fronds, part of a hibachi. But sometimes the net lives: baby Weke, Tang, Spanish Dancer, Puffer, Moorish Idol, and now, a spotted Cowfish that sits in my palms. It is smooth, hard and boxy. I hold it against my ear and stare at Glenn. Sounds like it's crying, I say. It's making these high beeps.

He takes the fish and strokes its sides, taps the horn, pretends to kiss its lips. "These make neat pets," he says. "If I had a fish tank, I'd keep one."

We talk about nothing, about everything. He tells me he can see through the white shorts and that the needlefish left small red dots on my thighs. He says I look better without eye shadow, and my hair looks nice when it's curled, and why did I wear opal earrings to go torch fishing? He slaps the water. "God," he says. "I never saw such perfect conditions as tonight!"

But you didn't catch anything, Glenn. Except a sea cucumber and the inner tube from some kid's bike.

He nudges me lightly with his spear and says, "I just caught a two-ton whale. A whale in short shorts."

"It's about eleven," Glenn says. "Let's go. Tide's coming in." I'm tempted to ask him to put out the light. I want to know what it's like to be a complete foreigner in this element I know well. I *thought* I knew well. Tonight was different—not fun—but different. Kind of like walking into church during mid-prayer.

Glenn puts an arm around my waist and says, "Tomorrow we'll stay as long as you want at Spats."

I nod absentmindedly. There must be at least five pounds of sand in each shoe . . . and boy, that was a cute Cowfish . . . and the way that lantern hovers over the water out there makes me think of the times we'd go camping and we'd be the only light on the mountain for miles.

Maybe Glenn'll buy me some rubber tabis for my birthday. Either that, or a wetsuit and my own net.

'Au 'A 'Ia

Mary Beth Aldosa

from *Bamboo Ridge* Issue #84, first aired November 10, 2009

Kumu sat on the steps leading to the stage at the Diamond Head end of Lehua School's cafeteria, the large wooden *pahu* drum completely filling the space between his legs. Despite opening the room's six swinging doors to their widest point, the air in the caf was hot and still. The breezes that usually wafted in to cool our *hālau*'s dancers seemed hesitant, not wanting to enter tonight. Was it the *pahu*'s presence or some other source of tension that hung in the air? The wind seemingly sensed what we *haumāna* knew: we were doing drum dances tonight. Hula was not going to be fun.

I threw my bag onto one of the cafeteria's long, white tables, pulling my blue calico *pā'ū* skirt over my work clothes. Everyone, it seemed, was in a bad mood, and I soon discovered it wasn't entirely because of the drum.

"Da nerve, yeah? Dat haole kid. You saw him on TV? Fricken atti*tude*!!" said Tanya, in disgust.

Jan's laughter spilled over into her words. "Das fo get cracks! And mo worse, braddah is on da football team! You *know* he goin' get lickens."

"It's not really the kid," added Cathy in her high-class pidgin. "It's the *mutha*. Hel-lo!! It states right on the application, BI-O-LOGICAL grandparents!"

I slid into line as Kumu let his thick hands fall simultaneously onto the drum's sharkskin surface.

"Alright, let's get started," Kumu called, pulling his drum closer to him. He lifted his hands again, pounding out familiar rhythms with the graceful hands of a dancer:

Oo te te te, oo te te.

Oo te te te, oo te te.

Kumu took us through the basic steps of the hula, calling out each new movement with perfect and practiced timing, "*Hela . . . 'ami . . . 'uwehe . . . kāwelu . . . kāholo . . . .*" Correcting his dancers, reminding and prodding us to push further, bend lower, fully extend the arm, the foot, the leg, all the while pounding out a steady drumbeat.

Oo te te te, oo te te.

"Girls, push out your *kīkala*!"

Oo te te te, oo te te.

"Flatten your foot, Malia."

Within minutes of "basics" my leg muscles began to ache and stiffen. My T-shirt, wet with sweat, clung to me and I struggled to catch my breath. Still, with calves that felt as though they were on fire, I repeated *hela* after *hela*.

Oo te te te, oo te te.

Finally, the drumming stopped, but our relief was short lived. "Alright everyone. Take a second, then we'll get started on 'Au 'A 'Ia."

Oh Lord! Not 'Au 'A 'Ia?! Just the thought of the dance's strenuous movements tired me. Dancers left their lines to grab water bottles or a bit of fresh air, stretching stiff limbs and trying to return their breathing to normal.

"Whoa! Extra long warm-ups, and now 'Au 'A 'Ia? Okay, which one of you guys went piss him off?" joked Alina, one of Kumu's old-timers. We giggled softly, which Kumu must have taken to mean that we had had enough of a break because he called us back to dance.

"Alright," Kumu began. "Who remembers what 'Au 'A 'Ia means?"

Even before most of us had fully processed Kumu's question, Yaeko was calling out the answer. At sixty-two, Yaeko was our oldest dancer and she knew all the answers. She studied every song, memorized every movement. While other dancers spent their breaks smoking cigarettes or talking story, Yaeko would diligently study her hula book. She'd taken hula for years and practiced daily. Despite her efforts, Yaeko was not considered a beautiful hula dancer. Still, what she lacked in gracefulness she more than made up for in knowledge and heart. The halau's younger dancers didn't appreciate this about Yaeko, but I did.

"Be . . . ah . . . steen-a-gee," she said, in her thick Japanese accent.

"Be stingy. Very good, Yaeko. Ladies, it was a warning, remember? A warning, to hold on to our culture, our way of life. Now, this motion." Kumu lifted his arms to shoulder height, extended his hands out toward us, and crisply and deliberately flipped them . . . palms up, palms down, palms up, palms down. Flip, flop, flip. "What is this motion supposed to signify?"

Finally, a question I could answer. "Turmoil," I said softly.

Kumu nodded. "Maika'i. Yes, the flipping of the hands represents turmoil. Remember now, this chant comes from a prophecy that things in Hawai'i were going to change. It was foreseen that people would come here, to these islands, and the change they brought would leave us in turmoil." He dropped his hands and looked at us. "Ladies, I expect to see that emotion in your dance."

Kumu walked back to his drum and sat on the steps facing his dancers. He raised his hands and let them fall. A series of low, loud thuds resounded through the room. I stood still, and felt my breath coming harder and faster, not from exertion since I had not moved a muscle, but rather, from rage. Frustration at the week's events, at Judge Ezra's decision to allow a non-Hawaiian into Kamehameha School, flowed through my veins, feeding each cell with a rage I rarely allowed myself to feel. The anger moved, danced to the pahu's beat, a slow-moving lava flow, deadly and unforgiving, Kumu Kula called to us, readied us for the dance.

"Ae, 'Au 'a 'ia e kama e kona moku . . . 'Au 'a!"

Weeks of conditioning had trained our bodies to respond almost automatically to Kumu's call, his *kāhea*. Hips began their slow circular motion, an *'ami* to the right that, once completed, was then reversed, becoming an *'ami* to the left. *Right . . . reverse, left . . . reverse*, the body moving, circling, dancing in an imitation of life: Hawaiians taking the same path but going nowhere, rounding a corner only to be pushed back. My heart pounded as I forcefully pushed and pulled at the air, grabbing, grasping. But for what? The motions were repeated, driven by the slow beat of the *pahu*, that with each repetition grew faster and more bombastic.

Nara Springer Cardenas reads "'Au 'A 'Ia"

"'*Ai ha'a!*" Kumu commanded loudly. "You need to *'ai ha'a!* Bend your knees!" The drumbeat came to an abrupt halt as Kumu stood.

"All of you," he said, "do this motion." We obeyed, imitating Kumu's hand placement, our right fists firmly sitting on our left.

"Now, from here, I want you to twist and push down."

Twist . . . push down. Twist . . . push down. Kumu observed the movment, still unhappy with its execution.

"No, that's not quite it," he said, more to himself than to the class. "Look, ladies, I need you to visualize. Think of someone you can't stand. Now, take your fists and make a wringing motion . . . like you're wringing their neck! Have you all got a person in mind?" Kumu asked mischievously.

Oh yes, Kumu, I thought. *I have a perfect someone in mind . . . a certain* maha'oi haole *from Kaua'i . . . a certain lying, non-Hawaiian "mutha" who sneaked her smug little brat into Kamehameha School . . . a certain scheming, lying little thief.*

Kumu made his way back to his drum, raised his hands, and let them fall with a thump. Right on cue, the dancers commenced, but within seconds, Kumu's drum fell silent again, bringing the dancers to a halt mid-motion. Our frustration manifested itself in the strange looks that passed between us. *What had we done wrong this time?*

Kumu stood up and walked out from behind the *pahu*. "Ladies," he said, a look of exasperation on his face. "*Think* about your dance. As a dancer, you need to think! What are you saying?!" His question lingered in the air. *What are we saying*, I thought.

"You folks wanna know what I see?" Kumu asked. "This is what I see."

He took what vaguely resembled the correct body position, his erect arms slackening, falling just an inch or two. His fully extended leg had been repositioned, bent as a prostitute on a street corner might do to attract a customer. And his hands had changed as well, converting from the desired harsh, stiff-fingered movements to the soft, languid hand movements that people generally associate with hula. Kumu repeatedly flipped his hands, a soft, gentle flip, smiling as he did so. *Palms up, palms down, palms up, palms down. Flippity, floppity, flip.*

Kumu spoke calmly. "When you do your motions to 'Au 'A 'Ia like this, this is what you are saying." When he spoke again, the pitch of his voice was higher and decidedly feminine, as were his mannerisms. "*Howzit . . . you like my land? Go 'head. Take 'em . . . How 'bout my cah? You like my cah too? Hea . . . hea da keys. Eh, by da way, you like come Kamehameha School? Come! It's all yoa's. Halp yo'salf!*" Kumu's stunned students erupted with laughter, as did he.

Finally, Kumu composed himself. "Ladies, that is not the message we want to send! We need to be strong, be stingy, *'au 'a 'ia* . . . we need to hold on! Let's try it one last time."

Kumu returned to his place on the steps, his tired hands and eyes rested on his *pahu*, as he lifted his hands and let them fall once more. Raising his eyes, he looked over the *pahu* at us, his voice poised to *kāhea*. And then I remembered. Kumu . . . our beloved kumu who gave so much of himself, who sought to empower his students through the dance, who unlocked the mysteries of our *kūpuna* . . . our revered kumu was not Hawaiian.

The commanding boom of the *pahu* startled me, and when I began to dance, I was a half step behind the others. I felt Kumu's eyes on me as I struggled to catch up to the class, to find my place in the dance, but in that split second, I had lost my focus. I paid dearly for my inattention, as all dancers do, for even as I danced, even as I grasped, pulled, and twisted, I felt it. In desperation, I reached out and tried to cling to it, but my rage, the rage that had once fueled my dance, continued to slip away from me. *I can't do this, Kumu,* I thought. *It's just not in me.* I danced in spite of the tears that were intent on coming, wanting to only dance through the pain and disappointment, wanting desperately for the dance to end.

When the final drumbeat sounded, it was Alina who spoke first.

"Kumu," she panted, "We could use a break. Whoa! Dat dance is killin' me!"

Kumu smiled and nodded silently, freeing his dancers to leave their lines. Most headed to the lanai outside the *makai* doors. I always preferred the quiet and dark of the *mauka* side of the building. I headed there and leaned my back against the cool metal of one of the lanai's orange poles. The material of my *pā'ū* skirt helped smooth the way, as I slid down the pole to the concrete floor and sat in the cool blackness. The voices of my fellow dancers seemed distant, and for tonight, I wanted to keep them there. I needed to be alone, to feel my own feelings, to know my own heart, not someone else's.

From where I sat, I could see the entire room. I watched silently as Kumu reverently lifted his *pahu* and gently placed it in the center of a large square piece of faded green fabric. He bent down to gather the cloth's four corners, wrapped the drum's sides, and tied the opposing corners into a knot, binding them tightly together. He slid his hands between the knotted fabric and the drum's surface, lifting the *pahu* from its place of honor at the room's center to a less prominent location off to the side. I heard Kumu's voice, lighter now, call to his *haumāna* to return to the room. It was time to begin the *'auana* portion of the night, the hula numbers that we always looked forward to. I watched as my fellow dancers lined up, but I couldn't bring myself to join them. I still had not fully recovered from *'Au 'A 'Ia*. I turned back to the night, and thought about Kumu, about the dance he had chosen for us, about a mother from Kaua'i and her son. What was it that I was supposed to take from tonight? What was the lesson?

I finally realized that, for me, *'Au 'A 'Ia* can never again be just another dance. It is a reminder, my reminder, to say vigilant, for change is coming, and it will keep coming. From a chant written over a century ago, generations before my mother and her mother before her, came a message from our *kūpuna*, as real and true today as it was then: *'au 'a 'ia* . . . hold on to your culture . . . hold on to your traditions . . . *'au 'a 'ia* . . . be stingy. And Kalena Santos, the mother from Kaua'i, source of the hurt and anger running through the Hawaiian community right now. What of her? Perhaps she was put in our path as a reminder as well . . . to remind every Hawaiian that the threat to our people is real. It lives and breathes and walks among us every day. The names will change, the faces will change, but they will always be with us. Which brings me to Kumu. He is a reminder as well, a loving reminder that not all non-Hawaiians will try to take from us. Some will love us, nurture us, and empower us. Some like Kumu will help us find our way back to our past, to the wisdom of our ancestors, without asking for anything in return but our love and friendship.

"*Meri Bet? You okay? Kumu send-a me to check on you.*" It was Yaeko. I smiled at her through my tears, and nodded. She extended her hand, and I took it gladly. Then she pulled me to my feet.

Puanani Burgess
writer

Aloha kākou.

Although "Hawai'i Pono'i" appeared first as a poem, it actually was a short story that recorded the actual happenings during an "excursion" to 'Iolani Palace on August 7, 1987. When I heard the poem performed on *Aloha Shorts* by Nara Springer Cardenas, the events of that day came alive again and I could feel the Queen's whispered prayer to me:

> *E Pua. Remember:*
> *This is not America.*
> *and we are not Americans.*
> *Hawai'i Pono'i.*

Amene.

Hawai'i Pono'i

Puanani Burgess

from *Bamboo Ridge* Issue #36, first aired November 17, 2009

On Friday, August 7, 1987,
Forty-three kanakas from Wai'anae
In a deluxe, super-duper, air-conditioned, tinted-glass, tourist-kind bus,
Headed to Honolulu on an excursion to the Palace, 'Iolani Palace.

Racing through Wai'anae, Maili, Nanakuli—
Past Kahe Point, past the Ewa Plain . . .

In the back of the bus, the teenagers, 35 of them,
Were rappin', and snappin', and shouting to friends and strangers alike:
        "Eh, howzit, check it out, goin' to town."

(Along the way, people stop and stare, wondering,
        What are those blahs and titas doing in that bus?)

Cousin Bozo, our driver (yes, that's his real name),
Spins the steering wheel,
Squeezing and angling that hulk-of-a-bus
through the gates made just
wide enough   for horses, and carriages, and buggies.

Docent Doris greets us:
"Aloha mai. Aloha mai. Aloha mai.
"Only twenty per group, please.
"Young people, please.
"Deposit your gum and candy in the trash.
"No radios. No cameras.
"Quiet. Please."

"Now, will you follow me up these steps.
"Hele mai 'oukou, e awiwi."

Like a pile of fish, we rush after her.
At the top of the steps,
We put on soft, mauve colored cloth coverings over our

shoes and slippers,
   to protect the precious koa wood floors
   from the imprint of our modern step.

Through the polished koa wood doors, with elegantly etched glass windows,
Docent Doris ushers us into another Time.

Over the carefully polished floors we glide through the
   darkened hallways: spinning, sniffing, turning, fingers
   reaching to touch something sacred, something forbidden
   —quickly.

Then into the formal dining room, silent now.
Table set: the finest French crystal gleaming; spoons,
   knives, forks, laid with precision next to gold-rimmed
   plates with the emblem of the King.
Silent now.

Laʻamea ʻū.

Portraits of friends of Hawaiʻi line the dining room walls:
   a Napoleon, a British Admiral . . . But no portrait of
   any American President. (Did you know that?)

Then, into the ballroom.
Where the King, Kalakaua, and his Queen Kapiʻolani, and their guests,
   waltzed, sang and laughed and yawned into the Dawn.
   (No one daring to leave before His Majesty.)
Now, as then, the Royal Hawaiian Band plays
   the Hawaiian National Anthem
   and the chattering and negotiating stop.
         The King and his shy Queen,
         descend the center stairway.

And up that same stairway, we ascend—the twenty of us.
Encouraged, at last, to touch . . .
      Running our hands over the koa railing
      . . . we embrace our history.

To the right is the Queen's sunny room . . . a faint
    rustle of petticoats.

To the left, we enter the King's study:

    Books everywhere. Photographs everywhere.
    The smell of leather, and tobacco, ink and parchment—
    The smell of a man at work.

    Electric light bulbs (in the Palace of a savage, can you imagine?)
    Docent Doris tells us to be proud, that electricity lit
    the Palace before the White House.
    There, a telephone on the wall.

    Iwalani longs to open those books on his desk,
    Tony tries to read and translate the documents,
        written in Hawaiian, just lying on his desk.

La'amea 'ū.

Slowly, we leave the King.
And walk into the final room to be viewed on the second floor.
The room is almost empty. The room is almost dark.
It is a small room. It is a confining room.
    It is the prison room of Queen Lili'uokalani.

Docent Doris tells us:
    "This is the room Queen Lili'uokalani was imprisoned in
    for nine months, after she was convicted of treason.
    She had only one haole lady-in-waiting.
    She was not allowed to leave this room during that time.
    She was not allowed to have any visitors or
    communications with anyone else.
    She was not allowed to have any knowledge of what was
    happening to her Hawai'i or to her people."

Liliuokalani 'ū.

    I move away from the group.

First, I walk to one dark corner, then another,
          then another. Pacing. Pacing. Searching.
          Trying to find a point of reference, an anchor,
          a hole, a door, a hand, a window, my breath . . .
I was in that room. Her room. In which she lived and
          died and composed songs for her people. It was
          the room in which she composed prayers to a
          deaf people:

          "Oh honest Americans, hear me for my down-trodden
          people . . ."

She stood with me at her window:
Looking out on the world that she would never rule again;
Looking out on the world that she would only remember
          in the scent of flowers;
Looking out on a world that once despised her.

          And in my left ear, she whispered:
          E, Pua. Remember:
          This is not America
          And we are not Americans.
          Hawai'i Pono'i.

Amene.

MUSINGS ON THE PAST

As we were preparing this anthology, new themes emerged as we revisited our favorites. Though these pieces were not originally recorded together, over the years, Bamboo Ridge writers have commemorated events, places, and people long gone from Hawai'i's cultural landscape. Here, we remember the 1946 Hilo tsunami with Juliet S. Kono, and Kahului's old Toda Drugstore with Michael McPherson. On a more personal note, in Wing Tek Lum's "A Wife Reminisces," the speaker relishes past passion, and in Marjorie Sinclair's "Lava Watch," an old woman sets memories in her heart before Pele claims her home. Kimo Armitage's "Uncle's Drum" was originally programmed under "Art & the Artist." Here the loss of art and creativity is mourned, but not forgotten.

A Wife Reminisces

Wing Tek Lum

from *Bamboo Ridge* Issue #73, first aired January 11, 2011

I bore him sons, and also daughters,
and though we love our children
we loved making them even more,
or so it seemed in those frantic young days
before we were married,
before we called ourselves husband and wife,
the dragon and the phoenix,
the needle and the flowers making sweet leis.

In those days we were like fledglings
hiding in the bosom of the banana grove
where the valley walls start their steep climb.
As soon as we were out of sight
he would be at my breasts,
my hands yanking down his pants in one swoop,
our bodies twisting and falling,
like fishhooks entangled,
like wrestlers caught in a deathly hold.
We would find that so worn spot on the ground.
He would cut a few large leaves
to place under me
so that my back would not get scratched,
he told me smiling.

Actually we did little talking,
our foreign tongues busy elsewhere
like our pecking fingers, our swollen thighs.
Often we would snuggle together on our sides,
he at my back nibbling on my ear lobes
—long ones which he believed
foretold my longevity—
driving me to distraction like an eel.
I would engulf his cane stalk nursing his sweet juices,
or he would enter me from behind
into the depths of my sand crab hold,

quickly, as if seized by our fear
that if this were all to life
we still could never get enough of it.

At other times he would suckle my nipple
for what seemed like half a day
and my breasts would open like wide eyes.
I loved his rump, smooth as the moon,
his curve without a flaw
like the curl of a perfect wave
so self-contained and mesmerizing.
I often raked my fingernails there
marking furrows in his skin
and always marveled at his resilience.
I taught him my secret names
for my body parts and his,
and his piercing eyes
would never stop following me
as I spread out beneath him like a pool.

Like a breadfruit blossom
my bud stood erect all day
waiting for his snout to root and prod.
I was the chili pepper burning his dark lips.
He drank me like a gushing spring
and I can still see his wink
feigning shyness as he leaned over
wiping his mouth
to whisper about my taste, salty and wet.

And then there were his eyes,
so dark and unwavering.
I made it a point each time
to fix my eyes on his as I came,
or I tried to, wild and gleaming,
then turning glazed at the point of no return
to carry him up into my dreams.

All I wanted was to live
those heedless moments as if forever
as if our little deaths would never die.

Soon we resolved to live together,
two large rocks standing in a forlorn sea.
His friends I know thought him crazy
from too much sex
and feared that he would never return then
to his land of flowers.
My mother banished me
even after he recited the proper speech
I taught him to say.
He was, she warned, a vagrant
trespassing our protected sea,
a plover who when his breast turned dark
would fly away.
The gourds were broken, never to be mended.

Like lovers of old,
we snatched embers from the fire
to scar our skin
as medals of our troth.

We rode sidesaddle
to the other side of the mountains
and lived by ourselves.
I taught him how to swim.
He taught me how to sew.
We each taught the other
kisses that neither of us thought we knew.

We farmed and foraged for our food by day.
As dusk I danced my hula for his eyes only
and he showed me secret martial arts sets
passed down from his heroes of long ago.
We would save our candlenuts
and as the moon rose
we would lie outside our lean-to

making love in the owl's light
the fingertips of the mountain breeze
tickling our skin.

Together we gathered pomegranates
and mountain apples in the shade.
We had our babies soon after
and our days became filled
with me and my stout belly
leaning over my taro patch,
he and our beloved chasing after his pigs.
But we would still have our moments
as when we would bring our small ones
to bathe at the mouth of the river
where it meets the sea.
Our naked bodies, dark as lava, would glisten,
and he and I would sit on the beach
one behind the other in turn
to braid each other's newly washed hair
with our memories of those heady, furtive days,
these cords of our common love.

(with phrases taken directly from Mary Kawena Pukui, ʻŌlelo Noʻeau, and Wolfram Eberhard, *Dictionary of Chinese Symbols*)

Tsunami: April Fool's Day, 1946

Juliet S. Kono

from *Hilo Rains*, first aired April 28, 2009

Sun-bleached houses
of Shin-machi line one end
of Hilo Bay
like crooked teeth.
Sampans creak and mar
the stillness of this
unsuspecting fishing village.
But soon sea birds take flight,
lecture their premonitions.
Groups of silence
spring to attention.

Curious, we bite
into the porch railing
with our bellies
and watch the tide recede.
Sleep-loosened hair
caresses our faces,
the morning air.
We hear a rumble far off;
something's coming in.
And before we know it,
a tsunami has us walled in.
The warnings come too late.
We children are hurriedly piggy-backed
by Aunt Miyoko and Mother.
Father rushes out
to start his Model-T.

Namu Amida Butsu.
Mother puts her hands together
in *gassho*. Water curls
above us like a tongue
lashing; it breaks apart the house.
The kitchen *tansu* crashes

with Mother's wedding china.
We lose sight of Grandmother.
We head out for the car
but we never make it.
We all link hands.
Reminded to breathe deeply,
warned to never let go,
we all go under.

The wave's force shoves us
this way and that.
Our *miki neko* drowns
clawing the last shriek
of the house. Things
sink in this widening mouth of water
foraging for the young and old,
those weak on their feet,
or in their will.
Life burdens us.
It seems easier to give up
and die. But when air bursts
into our lungs we grow hopeful.
We cling to things we can grasp.
We float with debris
and bodies whose whitened
and astonished faces
all look familiar.
We retch and gasp.

The tsunami tries three times
to gulp us into the mouth
of its watery womb.
Exhausted, finally,
the water subsides and ebbs
once more
mindful only of the moon.
The aftermath leaves people
dazed and horrified.

Flies come in hordes
to taste death.
People come to claim the bloated
bodies of relatives and friends.
Scavenger crabs run about
picking at flesh,
delighting in this new abundance,
while people collapse
in the solemn stench
of putting things to right.

Lava Watch
Marjorie Sinclair
from *Sister Stew*, first aired April 26, 2011

1.

The lava began to flow seven years ago and everyone talked about it. An appearance of Pele—her will, her power. No one thought to mention the danger to our village huddled under the green in the fragrances near the sea's edge; our village so old no one had heard when it began. Pele was—well, Pele: dictatorial, implacable. We listened to surf, not lava.

My whole body, however, quivered with that plume of smoke up the mountain and the red night flares. I smelt the lava seven years ago—a light sulfur odor mingling with faint fumes of burnt earth and burnt leaves. People said I was crazy. They said you couldn't smell those things so far down the mountain slope, and especially so near the sea.

Through the years the lava moved on with a leisurely insistence. It had a secret pace. Who could tell what was going to be: how far the molten rock would travel? Only Pele. Goddesses seldom reveal their thoughts. Their moods speak only at moments of action—unless they are in a prophetic mood. Pele was a goddess of action—a sudden appearance, clothed in fire.

On the mountain slope the lava has left a huge irregular trail of darkness, a trail of the burned and engulfed. People have moved from their burned homes hunting new lives wherever they can find them. Now the lava is at the village: relentlessly moving as if it had all the time in the world, its huge curling paws touching into flame everything in their way.

During those seven years, I passed my 70th birthday and two of my daughters left their husbands and moved back home. I reared a grandson who called my house home—whenever he was there. Samuel was a rascal boy, full of city ways. I wanted to give him the old country ways. He was always restless. He wouldn't stay. He was like a bird. The lava brought him back for a while, and he hiked through the woods to where he could see it, sometimes camping for several days. Of course he wasn't supposed to do that, but he was expert at escaping notice. I finally decided that I mustn't worry about him. Or even ask him where he went. I guess I can't blame him too much for his mercurial behavior. My parents thought I was that way when I was young. After all, I had disappeared into California for a while. I wish I could be that way now, flitting from place to place. But I'm stuck here sitting around with old age, with the girls, Piilani and Harriet. And the lava has almost reached my back door.

2.

Piilani was impatient with her mother's attitude toward the coming of the lava. Mom didn't want to do anything. Couldn't she see the inevitable? Couldn't she feel it in her bones? She simply drifted serenely from day to day, acting as if the lava moving down the mountain were a stream of water. She watched the houses burn. Afterwards she embraced her old friends, her neighbors, and cried with them; she even gave them shelter for a night or two. She was, however, tranquil and steadfast. And she wouldn't allow anyone to remove her things from the house. "The time has not come," she said. Yet the lava was almost up to the old stone wall great-grandpa had build long ago. The pond in the back yard had turned brown and seemed almost to be boiling. The water heaved, mud churning up from the bottom.

"Look, Mom, your pond is turning into lava," Piilani said. Red anger was in her face. "It's time. For god's sake, it's time!"

Keahi looked beyond her daughter at the stark lava softened by the green foliage of the plumeria and hau trees. At some moment the leaves and fronds would burst into torches. She was sure the trees knew by now. Just as her father and grandfather in their graves in the side yard knew. Grandfather always said: Pele gives and Pele takes away.

Harriet the younger daughter embraced her. "Mom, you're a little confused. I don't blame you. Why don't you let Pii and me take charge?"

Keahi returned the embrace, then broke away from Harriet's arms. She had her plans, very simple ones. But she wouldn't tell her children until the first paw of lava touched the house. Maybe not then, if she could manage.

"I'll go inside now if you want and look things over." She saw the brightening in her daughters' faces. It made her sad. "Some things I'll leave, the junk things."

In the living room she touched the pieces of old koa furniture. She laid her hands on the big table which had been polished by three generations. It was silky to the touch. She picked up one of the poi pounders from the shelf and saw, as she had so many times, her grandfather sitting in the back yard pounding poi on the big board. He had thin legs, a little pot belly and a head of thick white hair. She always thought it looked like sea foam. Long ago the board had disappeared. Now poi came from the market. She smiled slightly: change, change in everything—people, plants, even the shape of the mountain and the shore. Only the lava remained in its ancient ways, oozing or pouring from craters and vents as it made its slow passage, the trail of Pele down the mountain.

She went to the bedroom and lay down. These days she was often tired. Especially since the lava had come close. It was the unhurried pace of everything, the uncertainty; and she had to admit it, the anxiety. She hated anxiety. She knew exactly what would happen. When? That was what she asked as her heart beat irregularly and her breathing was heavy. She felt as if the lava were pulsing in her, a part of her. Sometimes she wanted to be part of it, treading slowly, stretching, breaking into red coals and flame: a moment of celebration. Afterwards, always a black collapse, a dark settling down.

"Hey, Mom, Mr. Lee is here." Tommy Lee was from Civil Defense. He had spindly legs like grandpa and teeth too big for his face. He was a good man. Very sympathetic, very tough, very fair. He walked into her room.

"Hello, Tommy, want something to drink?"

"No thanks. I came to see if you have made plans. I figure another 48 hours."

"You usually figure right."

"Thanks, Keahi. I ought to know. But then you can't always be sure."

"I'll get some boxes and start packing. The girls are pretty much packed. I think their friend is bringing a truck today."

"That's good. What about you?"

She laughed. "What about me? Well, what about me?"

"Your safety is my job."

He was a little pompous, she thought.

"Okay, save me." She flung out her arms.

He smiled and gently slapped her elbow.

3.

The truck has come, the house is full of people, confusion, noise. I'm out near the wall. The lava touches it in places. Intermittent snake tongues of flame reach out. Shrubs fire up and fill the air with smoke. The black paws seem reluctant to climb our small wall. They puff in redness, shoot out orange and blue, then collapse into darkness. The lava has its own voice—it crackles, even a roar that becomes a tinkling sound as momentary cooling begins. It is its own thing.

I remember the first time I smelled the lava. It was the 1935 flow up between the mountains. It was cold and the air pricked my nose. Still the lava smell was warm like sun on rock on a hot day. The fumes were sulfuric. The cold air muted everything. Down here by the sea the salty air mingles with the lava; strange odors, bitter and choking, filter through the air.

"Mom, where are you?" Harriet is bellowing. She's always had a raucous voice, deep as a man's. She's like a man, aggressive, demanding. At the same time she's beautiful in a large sort of way. Like her father, big eyes and glossy hair.

She knows perfectly well where I am. There's no place to hide. She likes to yell. That's all.

She is suddenly standing next to me. Her face is sweaty and her T-shirt stained with dust and grease. The outline of her breasts is round and strong. "Mom, where's your stuff? You haven't even started yet!"

"I'll get to it in my own time. Don't worry."

"The point is you have to follow the lava's time. It's going to burn us down."

"Hush, girl." I dread their rage, their resistance. Piilani's just the same. They can't accept what they can't control.

"Your time," she snorts. "We know what your time is. Well, it's your own problem."

She's back in the house and I'm alone again. It's good being alone. I like peacefulness. Before the lava came so close, I could lie down and have a nap. No one asked if I was okay. I could sit in a chair and rock, letting images of the past swarm before my eyes. I could even see the days in San Francisco before I gave up and returned to my village. For many years I never doubted my decision. Only in these last seven years I have. And I don't understand why. Could it be that I too hate the ravaging, uncontrollable lava, spoiling everything? All the changes, new plans for life; and just at a time when I want to settle down, sink a little into the green and the earth. Why should it happen? A simple technical answer. Tommy says we're in a rift zone. Sooner or later there would have to be lava. I chose village life with the possibility of a fire I had forgotten was living under that earth.

More than fifty years ago I walked up and down San Francisco streets with their hard cement, cold wind plastering my clothes to me and the shadow of tall stern buildings. In the afternoon the fog always came in. The fog helped a little, blurring the hard rectangular edges of things. I yearned for soft air, sea sound, the clatter of coconut fronds.

But more than that I yearned for people: the village people, taking things as they come, living in the moment, the day—not always looking to a future which would take place at an unknown time, maybe never. If they were angry, they shouted. If they loved, they hugged each other. If they were hungry, they ate. Of course they didn't much like change. Or the strangers coming in and trying to take their land and imitate their ways. They suffered, on occasion, from a somber melancholy.

In San Francisco I was becoming somebody else. I decided she wasn't what I wanted to be. If I had stayed there I would be crisp, business-like, money-minded, looking to the future. It might have been a good thing. I had a first-rate job. Everyone wondered why I suddenly resigned and went home. Who can say why now? Exactly why? I did it and that's all. Now the village for which I yearned is being devoured. And I don't have that whole other life I never lived. And so I go round and round as I did all those years ago. There will have to be another life. What?

"Hey, Mom!" This time it was Pii. "You can't stay here until the fire strikes the house. You've got to get your stuff together."

"Look, Pii, the lava has almost reached the top of the wall over there by the hala tree. You remember, we buried poor old Brownie under that tree."

"You talk like you're pupule. What are we going to do about you?"

"Just let me be crazy."

"Don't you understand the danger? After all the burned houses?" She muttered impatiently. "You should have stayed in San Francisco."

I was startled. Had she read my mind? I couldn't stop the tears. She put her arms around me. "I'm sorry," she said.

"What you said is good. The way the lava is good. Bursting through old, forgotten blocks."

4.

It's dark. Tommy comes to tell me that only this night is left. Tomorrow is the deadline. He asks if I need help—he'd send some men. I tell him no and kiss him on the cheek.

I can hear the lava rustling and belching along the wall. In one place it has gone over and a fat finger reaches toward the house. Darkness flames at moments from burning gas or burning trees. I get up and put some clothes in a bag. I hunt in the dark along the shelf of artifacts for the small stone bowl, once a lamp, and the small adze with a sharp edge. I hunt for the calabash my grandmother gave me. She had patched it in the old way. That's all I want to take. The other bowls, the poi pounders, the books and old fishing weights can stay. The furniture can stay. The refrigerator and stove, the rugs. I want to give them all to the lava, to Pele. She wants the village. It's hers. It's always been hers.

I walk around the house trying to fix myself in it forever. I, Keahi, forever in this old wooden house buried in lava. Of course the house will burn. It won't be a house—just a place where a house was. But the poi pounders might remain. And the fishhooks made of bone. Most things are fragile. Like this mountain slope continuously changing, like this very island with fire in its belly. With Pele.

It is dawn. Samuel is standing by my bed. I ask him where he comes from and he says Australia. I don't ask why he was in Australia.

"I heard our house was going to burn. I came to get you."

He pulls me from bed and puts my old robe around me. "Come on, Tutu, or Tommy will be after you."

We hurriedly eat some leftover poi and bits of cold fried fish. He makes steaming coffee.

He opens the kitchen door wide so we can watch the lava. It has reached the oldest plumeria tree. One paw stretches toward the garage.

"It's an octopus," I say.

"Eh, Tutu, you always make fancy talk. No need wash the dishes. The lava will."

Tommy Lee shouts from the front door. "Hurry up, you two."

Samuel takes my two small bags and ushers me toward the door. "You go ahead," I say.

He gives me a questioning look.

"I'll be coming. Don't worry."

I had remembered my kukui nut necklace. Papa made it for me. During his last years when the sadness settled on him and he drank all the time, he polished kukui nuts. One day he wrapped a strand of white kukui in a ti leaf and gave it to me. It wasn't for a birthday or a celebration. He just gave it to me and shuffled off to his little room in the shed. That night I wore it when we ate. He smiled. I was fourteen at the time. He died a year later.

Samuel shouts from the door. "I'm coming to get you."

"No need," I answer.

I take the kukui nuts from my drawer and join the two on the lanai. Samuel puts his arms around me. His pickup truck is out there on the road. Tommy's van is there. No sign of the girls.

"I want to watch," I say.

"Okay, if you let Sam take care of you," Tommy says.

They don't trust me. They have wild fantasies. I'm a mad old woman. Oh no, I whisper. I'm just Keahi at the moment when my house begins to burn. And I'm still inside. I put myself there last night. I'm inside with all the others who have lived there. I'm inside with all the thoughts I had in San Francisco—and after I came home. My life, quiet, drifting, is there, each moment of it moving into every other moment in the fire.

I grip Samuel's arm. The house is incandescent with flame—only its dark skeleton shows. The roof is crashing, the fire shouts and roars. I'm glad I left all those old things for it to have. The lava can take them away.

Samuel helps me climb into the truck. "The girls didn't want to watch," he says. "But they knew you would want to."

The house is taking a long time to go. Heavy smoke lingers, shadowing everything. It smells like wood and rock and garbage burning. I can't feel anything, I'm empty. It's frightening. Only my eyes watch the end of the house. The rest of me is somewhere else.

I turn away and put a hand on Samuel's thigh. "Where are we going?"

"Like we planned. The girls are at Aunty's, waiting."

"I don't mean that!"

Samuel races the engine of his car and starts off with a lurch. "Yeah, where the hell is any of us going?"

Toda Drug
Michael McPherson
from *Bamboo Ridge* Issue #57, first aired May 31, 2011

The druggist and his wife will retire this month,
closing the soda fountain and these glass cases
filled with tropical souvenirs, brass ashtrays
embossed with palm trees and other oddities
hidden in Kahului's aging original shopping mall.
For years I've come here to fill prescriptions,
as if somehow to replace what time takes away.
When I used to come weekly for a bedridden friend,
these kind people would wait for me after hours
till I could cross the island for his supplies.
She tells me now they might travel a little,
and attend to a neglected residential property.
Above the soda fountain counter is a row
of Meadow Gold sundae signs, these identical
to others I remember from Big Island soda shops
of my early childhood, chocolate and strawberry
and hot fudge, but here the pineapple is missing.
A collector has asked if he can have the signs
when these doors swing shut one last time.
Outside retirees gather on wooden tables
for checkers, fellowship and games of chance.
A young man blows the fallen brown leaves
with a machine strapped across his back.
Passing among them, I slow my walk to watch.
An old woman strides directly up to me
and asks can I spare the little she needs.
I reach into my pocket for whatever is there
and press the coins into her outstretched hand,
then turn back out toward late afternoon traffic.

Uncle's Drum
Kimo Armitage
from *Bamboo Ridge* Issue #79, first aired May 19, 2009

Uncle go to Mākaha Beach, darktime
and jams on his drums.

Aunty lets him go,
check out his creative side, besides
so romantic.
All her friends jealous.

   "Learn to play something,"

they tell their fat husbands.

Beach People always ask:
"Eh, what you playing?"

Then. Polite kine.
"I can play too?"

Then they try act. But,
nobody good like Uncle.
'Cause he get plenty
fruh-stray-tion.
He just play, and play, and play.

Then one day, police men come, and
take his music away. They throw,
"You bodering people," at him,
until he believe it.

   "Come over here again, and we'll put you in jail."

So he went one noddah beach.
And play. Soft kine.
Soft *kine*.

Until
he no can handle,
and play real loud again.

Then other people came.
And brought their drums.
And ukuleles.
And maracas.
And spoons.
And they make a band.

When Uncle comes home,
he plays with his kids.
He go to work.
He love Aunty like a teenager.
But, the cops find the new music.

Then he no go no more.
"No need," he say.
"Too much trouble," he say.
"Too much fruh-stray-tion," he say.

But sometimes, I see him
looking out the window.
Tapping his fingers—small kine.
When no one looking.
Seeing music dance on the windowsill.

Hina Kneubuhl reads "Uncle's Drum"

FROM ME TO YOU

Two years after our final live taping, Hawai'i Public Radio was still receiving listener comments asking for *Aloha Shorts*. The station had begun to produce a program of recorded performances in the Atherton Studio called *Applause in a Small Room*. Hosted by sound engineer, Jason Taglianetti, the common thread for this concert series was storytelling, with the musicians encouraged to tell the stories behind their music. HPR saw that a spoken-word event in the format of *Aloha Shorts* would be well received by their loyal listeners and bring variety to the Atherton season, so the co-producers were invited to submit a proposal.

"From Me to You" was our response to this request for a one-time hana hou—and to our own sense that we had something more to say. Once we had settled on the theme (the mode of address, as described in the introduction to this book), we quickly agreed that we wanted to explore further what had proven so effective for the Hawaiian Writers taping—integrating the music with the readings. In keeping with the *Applause* format, we also decided we wanted to hear a musician talk about the performances, and we were very happy when Jon Osorio agreed to serve as singer and host.

"From Me to You" had its lighter moments, and featured several audience favorites from our *Aloha Shorts* repertory of authors and actors, including Devon Nekoba and Daryl Bonilla reading Darrell H.Y. Lum's "Marbles" and Daryl interacting with an audience member during Lee Cataluna's "Rogelio Cabingabang A.K.A. 'DJ Stankmaster.'" But as readers will see in the selection of pieces that follows, in certain ways the show had developed a darker, more resonant tone, perhaps best represented in the mash-up of Darrell H.Y. Lum's "Letter to Honolulu" and Keola Beamer's "Honolulu City Lights." The lyrics of the well-known tune take on new poignancy and edge when heard together with Darrell Lum's words that "nowadays not like before . . . nowadays hard fo see where we going."

Dog

Tracee H. Lee

from *Bamboo Ridge* Issue #84, first aired May 3, 2015

You are a little pea-brain sister with a choke chain heart, useless as fear, frozen stiff on this oppressive, hot day, watching your big brother cry. Your dad has pushed him into the street, pushed him with two wide-spread palms, right at the chest, the way men do. Your brother is sobbing, he is eighteen, and he's mentally retarded. You don't really know what that means, not yet, but your friend once told you it's like being a dog—when he's eighteen, it's like he's only five in dog years. And he'll act five for a long, long time. They call him special. You wish someone would just give him a shot or some pills to make him better, but they tell you this is the kind of sick a doctor can't fix. Your other brother isn't special, he's normal like you. And here you are, the three of you and your dad, on this hot day in Pearl City. You wonder why they call it Pearl City because there are no pearls anywhere. But you like it because your grandparents live here, and people have lots of pets and lots of barefoot kids your age. They even have an ice cream truck with Missiles, Melonas, Big Eds, and Choco Tacos with the crunchy shell. But this is no time for ice cream, because there is a scratch on the brand new Olds. It looks like a thumbnail, or a half moon. *I didn't do it, I don't know* you all plead. But your dad has already decided who put that little moon there. He looks crazy like a wolf with black in the eyes and you wish you were dead already. You wish you could burn in hell and take your brother with you. Your dad is yelling *goddam piece of shit what the hell fucking hell stupid asshole goddam lolo*. Your dad's face is red, the sky is red, everything's red like an old picture and you wish you were there already—way, way in the future and only looking back at this dumb old picture. You can't move. Your brother is crying, making little animal noises and you wish he would stop. Your dad has pushed him in the chest, the way men do. You don't move. You want to die.

Lamb

You are a silly excuse of a brother, it makes you laugh. Someone should have stamped you out with their thumb. Instead you are here, the second child, the leader by default. Here are your pets: this broken boy and this weak girl. You have not chosen this, this relentless sun heating the driveway with rusting car parts in front of this yard in Pearl City. Your grandfather waters the lettuce here in the mornings. But you cannot think of that, not now, because your father has pushed a retarded boy, your brother, into the street. Gravel leaps up around their ankles. Your father is mad again, a mad bear, savage and fierce. You imagine him on all fours, attacking. But this is no jungle, this is here, next to the plumeria tree in front of your grandparents' house. This man is your father, your half-self, you have the same name and the same hands. You wonder what kind of animal you will become. He has seen the scratch on the seat of the brand new Olds. No one knows who put it there but that doesn't matter now because your brother is sobbing, not like a child with a skinned knee, but something much worse. And here you are, your brother's shepherd until now. For a split second you imagine yourself quietly turning around, walking away from this tragedy beside the lettuce. You wish these people were TV actors, you do not know them, they are not a part of you. There is even a glass screen separating you from them. But instead you are frozen by your own fear, and your brother is shivering now. It's ninety degrees. He cries too because you have not come yet, where are you, he pleads. He is choking on his tears and swallowing, making little animal noises. You are supposed to be some sort of hero, and you think about all the other bullies at school, at the movies, on the bus that you've fought off. *At least there's that,* you think. But in the broad light of this July afternoon, in front of the sidewalk where the three of you once placed a footprint in new cement, you cannot even be the brother you are, and you wonder how many more little deaths he can survive without you.

Bug

You are a reasonable father, and the god of this fiasco. You are the keeper of these cowardly boys, this wayward girl. Your oldest one is slow, retarded, and this is not your fault. It's not anyone's fault, it just is. You are sweating in front of your parents' house and everything feels like heat rushing at you, the way the kids fought on the drive over, your back melting into the new leather, the heat rising from the gravel, lack of sleep. You finally saved enough money to buy a new car, and here it is finally, gleaming. And now someone has scratched the seat already. Isn't there something you can call your own? Sometimes you imagine leaving for work and never coming back— tiptoeing quietly away from their gentle breathing in the half-light of the morning. But somehow their images will follow you where you go, like a rain cloud, or a school of fish—those children—swimming after you! So here you are with three oblivious children under this blazing sun in the very spot where you were once fourteen. You've felt fourteen for as long as you can remember, even now. Has it really been thirty years, you think, since you first rode your new orange bike up this path? Was it thirty years since you dug up the red soil so the plumeria tree could be planted? Is it here that you remember your father barking orders at you, telling you *can't you even dig a hole right?* You remember his anger and the unforgiving sun on your backs. *Goddam good fo' noting son, you,* he says, and shoves you aside grabbing the shovel. You recall the red heaps of dirt he flung at your feet without looking. Later you remember that everything was stained red for a long time, even your skin. But all of this is silly now, because your children have no idea what fear is, what work is. They must be taught, it must be. You are a lion tamer, they are lions, it is natural, it must be. You did not ask for this retarded boy, but here he is before you, sweating and crying like a pathetic animal, and you must do what is necessary. Discipline is the only way, you think. You want him to grow up, so you treat him like a man, and you have pushed him, and you wish you hadn't, because now you see he is just a child, a tiny child, a tiny bug in the hand. But now it's too late, and it's happening again, *oh god,* you think, it's happening again, and you are saying things you don't even recognize and your children's eyes are on you, the sun is on you, and you wish you were somewhere else far away, somewhere blue, in the middle of the ocean and there would be water, just endless water everywhere you look, just blue, blue, blue.

For Robin, Unclaimed
Darlene M. Javar
from *Bamboo Ridge* Issue #100, first aired May 10, 2015

Thin as hibiscus petals—
sick for a month, unable to breathe,
you finally went to the emergency room,
but no one accompanied you
when you were transported
to the next hospital sixty miles away.
Not wanting you to be alone
I drove to Hilo Medical Center
and claimed we were related.
You talked through your oxygen mask
until the doctor came in and reported—
disease had claimed your body.
I used the phone at the nurse's counter
to call your home,
to tell your lover to hurry, to get here.

Unable to breathe,
again you were transported
to another hospital an island away,
again unaccompanied,
again unclaimed.

I called your mother after searching the directory,
explained I was a new friend,
acknowledged your absence of seven years;
the mother who once saved you,
adopted you, sheltered and loved you
when you were her little boy.
She told me you were already
damaged beyond repair
by the time she got you,
that she had lost you twice—
she calling you by her chosen male name,
me calling you by your chosen female name,
both of us not claiming your birth name;

and then the daughter she could not accept
disappeared for seven years.
"*Terminal, Saint Francis Hospital,*" I reported
then she contemplated
flying across the Pacific
to see you, to help you, to love you.

Your mother and I talked each week
and she shared
that she would sing to you over the phone,
love you, pray with you,
and she would come.

I called your friend in Alaska and shared with her
that you were dying. She said she would come,
to see you, to help you, to love you.
Each week we talked and she was still coming.

I called the transgender support group.
I called the nurse to complete your forms.
I called the doctor when you wanted to lessen the pain.

Flown to Oʻahu, an island away,
your lover said he would come,
to see you, to help you, to love you.
When the doctor called me
to say that you might not
make it through the night,
I bought the airline ticket for your lover,
so you wouldn't be alone and unclaimed anymore.
After a week, you sent him home.

When the doctor called me and said you had died,
I called your friend, your lover, your mother.
Alaska wanted your body, Arizona wanted your body,
but Oʻahu had your body.

A month after you pulled
off your oxygen mask,

two months after
you were admitted with AIDS,
a voice over the phone explained,
"Unclaimed bodies are incinerated."
Like you changed your name,
I changed my number.

Letter to Honolulu
Darrell H.Y. Lum
from *Bamboo Ridge* Issue #104, first aired May 10, 2015

Eh Honolulu,

Nowadays not like before. Not dat before was so hot either but I tink nowadays actually stay jes like before. Nowadays get plenny people working one two tree jobs fo buy something dey tink dey need. My mahdah, used to tell me, "No need. What fo?"

Before time was same: people work hard fo buy one house, fo go Mainland 'cause anyting Mainland was bettah. McDonald's. Color TV. Coors beer. We wasn't America. America was da Ed Sullivan really "Big Shew" on Sunday nights after we pau eat. One week delay. We was always one week behind. We was behind: neva going Disneyland, neva going see snow.

And now we still chasing da Mainland. Broke down Sears fo put one Bloomingdale's. Dey going broke down da Farmers Market fo put up 25 million dollar penthouses. Some guys tell, "How come dey no fix da stink first?" Sometimes da sewer smell come up from someplace but dey no can figgah out from where. "Ass okay," dey tell, "da trade winds blow um away most times." Except when get Kona weather. Da stink no blow away. Da vog come and da stink stay. My fahdah used to go Farmers Market fo buy chicken and da butcher give him one bag chicken feet fo free. Not stink.

Eh Honolulu, we still on da plantation. Nowadays still get plenny luna. Still get people who shame of who dey are. Still get people who telling us who we are. Still get people who only see da dollars. And still get <u>us</u>, who tell, "Yes Boss," when McGarrett say, "Book um Danno." Nobody on TV tell McGarrett, "Eh, you chasing da crook da wrong way around da island when he going airport. Eh, Wo Fat is da name of one restaurant not one crook." And we give four million dollars to da guys fo bring one junk pro football game to da Aloha Stadium, 'cause we no mo nutting bettah and it's good for us.

Governor Burns, one time, he said dat da problem was 'cause we stay shame, dat we no need be shame. I know what he mean. From small kid time, we was country, no class. Primo not as good as Coors. Lucky if you get one uncle work airline he can sneak in couple cases. McDonald's hamburger bettah den Chunky's 'cause get special sauce and 100% all beef. But when you put day-old bread, onions, and egg inside, come mo juicy, j'like da kine at KC Drive Inn or Likelike. Da old timers shake their head and say, "Nowadays not like before." Dey grumbo, grumbo, grumbo, and tell, "Ah, no can help. Progress dat." But nowadays if you no like something, you hold sign and shout, "La, la, la, la . . . I no can hear you!" Das why I still shame. Not about outsiders or insiders. I shame dat we no can say, "You right and I right. And what we going do?"

'Cause in da end, we live on one <u>island</u>. We ain't going nowhere.

Nowadays hard fo see where we going, 'cause no can see da road nighttime. Somebody went steal da copper wire.

See you,
Daro

Honolulu City Lights
Keola Beamer

Looking out upon the city lights
And the stars above the ocean
Got my ticket for the midnight plane
And it's not easy to leave again

Took my clothes and put them in the bag
Try not to think just yet of leaving
Looking out into the city night
And it's not easy to leave again

Each time Honolulu city lights
Stir up memories in me
Each night Honolulu city lights
Bring me back again

You are my island sunset
You are my island dream

Put on my shoes and light a cigarette
Wondering which of my friends will be here
Standing with their leis around my neck
It's not easy to leave again

Each time Honolulu city lights
Stir up memories in me
Each night Honolulu city lights
Bring me back again
Bring me back again

The company of "From Me to You"

An Image of the Good Times

Wing Tek Lum

from *Bamboo Ridge* Issue #44, first aired March 3, 2009

It would be at dinner
when I was just a kid
when my brothers were away in college
and there were just three of us
around our small table in the kitchen
my mother sitting to my right
and my father to the right of her
—that is, sitting opposite me
with his back to our chopping block.
And we would be finishing our meal
our rice bowls empty
our chopsticks and spoons laid on our plates
the dishes on our lazy susan
waiting to be cleared.
And my father would turn to the bunsen burner
hooked up to a spigot by the counter.
In a stainless steel pot
he would bring water to a boil.
In turn the water would be poured
into a small clay pot
he had stuffed full of his favorite leaves.
While waiting for his tea to brew
he would raise his leg
resting its heel against the edge of his chair
his thigh tucked into his chest.
He would reach over
underarm supported by his knee
to pour the tea into his cup.
The cup, saucer and pot were a matching set
and we learned over the years
never to wash them
to add to the dark pungency.
He would finish off the tea
in large, measured gulps

smacking his lips at the end
with a loud sigh of satisfaction
as if it could echo
against the chaos of the world
that reigned outside our home
outside of that love that bound us together
through our bad times and all the good.

Acknowledgments

For nearly ten years, the radio program *Aloha Shorts* made its home on the air and in the studios of Hawai'i Public Radio. Now, years later, HPR's audio archives make possible the digital recordings that accompany this collection. We are endlessly grateful to this independent radio station, its staff, donors, and listeners for their material and intangible support. Special recognition must also go to *Aloha Shorts'* sound engineer, Jason Taglianetti, who week after week shepherded our often unruly theatrics into coherent stories in sound. And to HPR volunteer house manager Sheryl Lynch, who shepherded our burgeoning audiences into the intimate Atherton Studio, somehow always finding a seat for everyone.

Aloha Shorts was always, first and foremost, a way to showcase Hawai'i's talented writers, actors, and musicians. A tall mahalo to the hundreds of individuals who so freely lent us their words, their voices, their music, their time, their artistry. This would include our Associate Producer Daniel Akiyama, a talented playwright in his own right, who lent us his quiet support in a myriad of ways—including introducing our audiences to his mother's homemade cookies. You all (and the cookies) will be remembered.

Bamboo Ridge Press has been at the forefront of developing Hawai'i's literary voices since long before *Aloha Shorts* came on the scene, and it continues after we have signed off. Were it not for the passion and vision of Bamboo Ridge co-founders Eric Chock and Darrell H.Y. Lum, staff members Wing Tek Lum and Joy Kobayashi-Cintrón, and their fiercely dedicated core of volunteers, *Aloha Shorts* and *The Best of Aloha Shorts* would truly not have come into being. Before we stepped up to the mics, there was your inspiration. Thank you very much.

— SC, CH, PL

Aloha Shorts Producers,
The Best of Aloha Shorts Editors

Sammie Choy is a Honolulu director, producer, and teacher. She received an MFA in Directing and a PhD in Theatre from the University of Hawaiʻi at Mānoa and currently teaches theatre and acting at Kapiʻolani Community College. Before returning to Hawaiʻi, she was a professional actor in the San Francisco Bay Area. For the past nine years, she has directed and produced living history productions on Oʻahu and Maui for the Hawaiʻi Pono'ī Coalition. She

Aloha Shorts producers from left to right Sammie, Craig, and Phyllis

is a past member of Kumu Kahua Theatre's board of directors and is active in fiber arts as a craftsperson and artist.

Craig Howes is a Professor of English, a co-editor of *Biography: An Interdisciplinary Quarterly*, and the Director of the Center for Biographical Research at the University of Hawaiʻi at Mānoa. With Jon Osorio, he co-edited *The Value of Hawaiʻi: Knowing the Past, Shaping the Future* (UH Press 2010). The series scholar and a co-producer for the *Biography Hawaiʻi* television documentary series, regularly screened on PBS Hawaii, he has served on the boards of Kumu Kahua Theatre and the Hawaiian Historical Society. He has appeared in many plays, including regularly in the Hawaiʻi Pono'ī Coalition *Mai Poina* Living History productions.

Phyllis S.K. Look has had a 20-year career in the theatre as an actor, director, teacher, and producer. She received an MFA in directing from Yale School of Drama, a National Endowment for the Arts/Theatre Communications Group Directing Fellowship, and a Poʻokela Award. She was a member of Berkeley Repertory Theatre's artistic staff and founded the Theatre's award-winning Education and Outreach Program. Her directing credits include productions at Berkeley Rep, the Kennedy Center, Lincoln Center Institute, Seattle Children's Theatre, Young Playwrights, and Sundance Children's Theatre, among others. She is currently the Director of Marketing at Hawaiʻi Public Radio.

Contributors

Mary Beth Sua Aldosa (1965 – 2007) is remembered for her melodious voice and her heart of gold! Her love of children led to a career in teaching; however, her passion was always music. She sang on two Brown Bags to Stardom albums and started the first children's choir at Saint Joseph's School in Waipahu. Her singing was always an expression of pure goodness and her loving, kind spirit. Her gifts—teacher, singer, amazing writer of poetry and short stories, loving daughter, sister, aunty, and friend—are treasured by all who were blessed to know her. But what she treasured most were her children: Kipeni, Kalani, Lolena, and Libby, and her husband Leonard.

Kimo Armitage has authored 24 books, mostly for children, in Hawaiian and in English. His recent novel, *The Healers*, was published by the University of Hawai'i Press. In 2016, he won the prestigious Maureen Egan Writers Exchange Award for Poetry, which is administered by Poets & Writers of New York City. In 2017, he won the Wax Poetry Art Socially Engaged Poets Award in Canada and published poems in *Fishfood, Eunoia Magazine, Cold Noon Journal, Cape Rock Literary Magazine, Bayou Magazine, Barking Sycamores*, and *Adelaide Literary Journal*.

Keola Beamer is a singer-songwriter and guitar master, one of the first to use Hawaiian slack key techniques in compositions that are at home on jazz or classical stages. He led the wave of contemporary Hawaiian music in the 1970s when he wrote "Honolulu City Lights" and authored the first slack key guitar instruction book. Keola has received the Hawai'i Academy of Recording Arts Lifetime Achievement Award, multiple Grammy Award nominations, and multiple Nā Hōkū Hanohano Awards. He is a Native Arts and Cultures Foundation Fellow, Artistic Director of the Mohala Hou Foundation, and President/Executive Director of Aloha Kuamo'o 'Āina, a nonprofit formed for the protection and preservation of the Kuamo'o Battlefield and Burial Grounds in Kona, Hawai'i.

Puanani Burgess is a designer and facilitator for Building the Beloved Community, a community building and conflict transformation process that brings people face-to-face for ceremony, storytelling, and circles of trust and respect. A published poet, mother, aunty, and friend to many, she is also one of the founders of several non-profit organizations, including the Wai'anae Coast Community Mental Health Center, Ka'ala Farm, Inc., Hoa 'Āina O Mākaha, and the Pu'a Foundation. She has served as the Myles and Zilphia Horton Chair for the Highlander Research and Education Center in Tennessee and as a community scholar in residence at the Department of Urban and Regional

Planning at the University of Hawai'i. She is an ordained Zen Buddhist priest in the International Daihonzan Chozen-ji.

Lee Cataluna is a Hawai'i-based writer. She is the metro columnist for the *Honolulu Star-Advertiser* and an award-winning playwright with more than a dozen production credits. Her collection *Folks You Meet in Longs* and her novel *Three Years on Doreen's Sofa* both received awards for Excellence in Literature from the Hawai'i Book Publishers Association. In 2004 she received the Cades Award for Literature for her body of work. She served as Keables Chair in creative writing at 'Iolani School.

Denise Duhamel's most recent book of poetry is *Scald* (Pittsburgh, 2017). *Blowout* (Pittsburgh, 2013) was a finalist for the National Book Critics Circle Award. Her other titles include *Ka-Ching!* (Pittsburgh, 2009); *Two and Two* (Pittsburgh, 2005); *Queen for a Day: Selected and New Poems* (Pittsburgh, 2001); *The Star-Spangled Banner* (Southern Illinois University Press, 1999); and *Kinky* (Orhisis, 1997). Duhamel is a recipient of fellowships from the Guggenhiem Foundation and the National Endowment for the Arts. She is a professor at Florida International University in Miami.

Derek Ferrar was born in New York City, lived as a monk in India, and found home in Hawai'i in the 1980s. He's worked as a writer, editor, and communicator for *Honolulu Weekly*, *Hana Hou!* Magazine, the Office of Hawaiian Affairs, and the East-West Center, among others. As a musical hobbyist, the highlight of his quasi-career so far was performing regularly for Hawai'i Public Radio listeners as a front man and multi-instrumentalist for the quirky *Aloha Shorts* house band, Hamajang, along with co-conspirators Charley Myers, Mark Scrufari, and Yash Wichmann-Walczak. Visit them at **HamajangBand.com.**

Jozuf "bradajo" Hadley: Born and raised in the early thirties on Kaua'i, it was on the playground at elementary school where my multi-ethnic classmates and I communicated in the grassroots Hawai'i folk talk called Pidgin. In the summer of 1969, while earning a master's degree in sculpture at UHM, three friends and I climbed down into Waimea Canyon, where I experienced an epiphany. Very shortly after this, a phonetic cursive flowed through me that represents a written form of this spoken-only language of Pidgin. My first book of this calligraphy, accompanied by my recorded narration, appeared in 1972 and was entitled *Chaloookyu eensai* (Try Look You Inside). **jozufhadley.com**

Mavis Hara: Thank you to the editors of *The Best of Aloha Shorts* for reaching a new audience for local literature.

Gail N. Harada is the author of *Beyond Green Tea and Grapefruit*, a collection of poems and stories (Bamboo Ridge Press, 2013). When she wrote "Waiting for Henry" she was very allergic to cats, but her allergy miraculously disappeared when she adopted a stray kitten a few years later.

Darlene M. Javar lives in the beautiful country of Kaʻu on the Big Island of Hawaiʻi. She has been published in *Bamboo Ridge, Hawaiʻi Pacific Review, Chaminade Literary Review, Tinfish, Kaimana, Storyboard 8, Into the Teeth of the Wind, The Distillery, Earth's Daughters*, and *The East Hawaii Observer*.

Lisa Linn Kanae is the author of the short story collection *Islands Linked By Ocean* (Bamboo Ridge Press) and *Sista Tongue* (Tinfish Press), a memoir/essay which weaves the social history of Hawaiʻi Creole English with personal experience. She is a recipient of the 2009 Elliot Cades Award for Literature and teaches at Kapiʻolani Community College.

Nora Okja Keller is the author of *Comfort Woman* and *Fox Girl*.

Born and raised in Wahiawā, **Stephanie Keiko Kong** travels the world as a yoga teacher, blogger, and performer. Stephanie is known for her compelling voice, which *Hana Hou!* Magazine calls "pitch-perfect pidgin," as she has brought to life the characters of many favorite local writers, including Lee Cataluna, Lisa Linn Kanae, Lois-Ann Yamanaka, and Hailiʻōpua Baker. She also meditates daily, does CrossFit, and would love to meet your mom.

Juliet S. Kono is the author of several books: *Hilo Rains, Tsunami Years, Hoʻolulu Park and the Pepsodent Smile, The Bravest Opihi*, and *Anshū*, a novel. She co-authored two collections of linked poetry, *No Choice but to Follow* and *What We Must Remember*. She has appeared in many anthologies and collections and is the recipient of several awards. She is retired and lives with her husband in Honolulu.

Lanning C. Lee was born and raised in Honolulu, Hawaiʻi. Except for some school in Madison, Wisconsin, he has lived in Honolulu all his life. He recently retired and has been spending much of the time traveling the world. There are no cockroaches in his home anymore. Combat® does a very good job.

Tracee H. Lee is a writer from Hawaiʻi residing in Seattle, Washington. She is currently working on stories about the lives of her grandparents.

Darrell H.Y. Lum, along with co-founder and co-editor Eric Chock, served for 37 years during the horse and buggy days of literary publishing before handing the reins over to new editors in 2015. They brought modern technology to Bamboo Ridge: radio! How great is that!

Wing Tek Lum is a Honolulu businessman and poet. Bamboo Ridge Press has published his two collections of poetry, *Expounding the Doubtful Points* (1987) and *The Nanjing Massacre: Poems* (2012).

Mark Lutwak used to play keyboards for Kupaʻāina. He still plays the accordion and lives with the playwright Y York in Seattle.

Michael McPherson (1947-2008) was born in Hilo, obtained his B.A. (1974) and his M.A. (1976) from the University of Hawaiʻi at Mānoa. He edited and published the literary journal *HAPA* on Maui (1980–83), was *Hawaii Review*'s first fiction editor (1972), and founded Xenophobia Press in Wailuku (1980). He authored a poetry collection, *Singing with the Owls* (Petronium Press, 1982); a novel, *Rivers of the Sun* (South Point Press, 2000); and *All Those Summers: Memories of Surfing's Golden Age* (Watermark Publishing, 2004). His poetry, short fiction, essays, and reviews appeared regularly in Hawaiʻi literary journals and anthologies. He was also a published legal scholar and practicing attorney in Hawaiʻi from 1991 to 2008.

Since the publication of his novel *ʻEwa Which Way*, **Tyler Miranda** has spent the last four years developing new English tropes, such as understated hyperbole, triple entendre, and straight-up irony. His latest project is the wordless haiku. Here's his favorite:

Devon Nekoba first "caught the bug" in high school from renowned theatre director Ron Bright and continued performing while at Gonzaga University. Upon returning home, he became involved with Kumu Kahua Theatre, performing at the University of Hawaiʻi and in numerous productions of Lisa Matsumoto's pidgin fairy tale trilogy, as well as in her traveling educational shows and later works. He has done commercials, been cast in *Hawaii Five-O*, *The Inhumans*, and local movie projects, most recently *Go for Broke*. He is currently the morning show host for 94.7 KUMU radio. He considers himself supremely blessed to have been a part of an amazing show like *Aloha Shorts* and thanks his wife and two wonderful children who allow him opportunities to "go and play."

Paris Priore-Kim began to tell stories when she was a high school student at Punahou School. She was mentored by a number of amazing storytellers throughout her life, beginning with her father. Another of those mentors, Phyllis Look, caught up with her much later in life and invited her into the *Aloha Shorts* 'ohana. For the last two decades, Paris has been an educator at Punahou School, where she revels in the stories all around her.

N. Keonaona (Aea) Russell: Thank you for including "Bearing the Light" in this collection. Because writing is about truth, discovery, and surprise, it remains my net that captures life's awesome details.

Aito Simpson Steele was born and raised on the island of Oʻahu. He has lived in Town for 90% of his life—Makiki, Nuʻuanu, Puʻunui, Kaimukī, and depending on how you look at it, ʻAiea. He is in no particular order a father, husband, son and performer, appearing sporadically on stage at Kumu Kahua Theatre and Honolulu Theatre for Youth, among others. He is currently most recognizable as a guy who changes light bulbs, trims hedges, hangs out at a fire pit, and tells stories.

Marjorie Putnam Sinclair Edel (1913-2005) was a poet, novelist, biographer, and teacher who made lasting contributions to Hawaiʻi's literary communities. She arrived in Honolulu on the University of Hawaiʻi's first graduate exchange student program in 1935. She was the author of two novels, *Kona* (1947), and *The Wild Wind* (1950); a biography, *Nahiʻenaʻena: Sacred Daughter of Hawaiʻi* (1976); and numerous poems and short stories reflecting the native Hawaiian experience in the early 20th century. In addition to teaching in the UHM English Department, she worked closely with the Hawaiʻi Literary Arts Council for over 25 years. Marjorie Edel received the Hawaiʻi Writer's Award in 1981.

Cedric Yamanaka is the author of *In Good Company*, a collection of short stories. He is a recipient of the Helen Deutsch Fellowship for Creative Writing from Boston University, the Ernest Hemingway Memorial Award for Creative Writing from the University of Hawaiʻi, and the Cades Award for Literature. He is currently working on a novel.

Lois-Ann Yamanaka is the Director of Naʻau Learning Center. She is currently working on her next book, *Up the Rabbit Hole*.